Returning in Glory

She looks in the mirror and feels betrayed by the fluorescent lights around it. The smudges under her eyes are darker than usual, and she's breaking out again. She pulls her makeup bag from her backpack and goes to work. In fifteen minutes or so, she looks more like her old self.

"Thank heavens for Cover Girl," she says aloud, giving her face in the mirror a parting pat before opening the bathroom door.

She drifts into thinking about the reunion, and about seeing her oldest, closest friends. Sweet dumb Leigh. Superwoman Sue. Scooter the madman. And, of course, Graham.

Graham. At the thought of him Jordan slides into deep daydream, the same one she's been having all week, ever since she decided she *would* come to the reunion, even if she wasn't returning in glory. The dream is a replay from the highlight tape of her life — the last time she saw Graham.

Look for these and other Point® Paperbacks
in your local bookstore!

Saturday Night
   by Caroline B. Cooney

Blind Date
   by R. L. Stine

The Karate Kid: Part II
   by B. B. Hiller / Robert Mark Kamen

SpaceCamp
   by Joe Claro / Larry B. Williams

HIGH SCHOOL REUNION

Carol White

SCHOLASTIC INC.
New York Toronto London Auckland Sydney

ISBN 0-590-33579-0

12 11 10 9 8 7 6 5 4 3 2 1   6   6 7 8 9/8 0 1/9

Chapter 1

Jordan looks idly out the window at the passing landscape, which has been changing grad-
ually from an industrial scene of water tanks
and slag heaps and refineries to a rural one
of pastures and farm fields, as the train heads
into Massachusetts.

She's going home, to Jamesburg. This
weekend is the one-year-after reunion of her
class at Jamesburg High. She had planned
to take this event by storm, to come back
from her year in New York a big star. But
that hasn't quite happened.

The blurring speed of the train and the
dark green tint of the glass and the Keith
Jarrett tape on her Walkman make her feel
isolated from this passing scene, as if it were
a movie, instead of reality. She feels like this
a lot lately.

Especially about her own life, which is
beginning to look like one of those late-night
tv movies about the small-town girl desper-
ately trying to make it in the Big City. She

feels like she's the star of this picture, but someone else is writing the script. And it doesn't look like it's moving toward a particularly happy ending.

She sighs and looks out the window again and tries not to think about how hungry she is. She's hungry pretty much all the time now. But she really shouldn't eat. No matter how many yogurt lunches and skipped dinners she has, it seems like all the other actresses at auditions are thinner than she is. If it weren't for the pills from Dr. Don, she wouldn't be able to compete at all.

It was her roommates — Nell and Tina — who turned her on to Dr. Don. They both get diet pills from him, too. The three of them are so hyper all the time now that most nights they play Trivial Pursuit until dawn. Then they get up at seven to make up for casting calls. Then they go to work — Jordan and Tina are waitresses, Nell drives a cab — until late at night. Jordan has been keeping up this pace for about six months now. When she got to the city, her dream was to find fame and fortune. Now her dream is being able to eat four Big Macs and then go to sleep for three days.

It's not exactly the life she imagined last spring, after graduation when she headed for New York to "follow her star." All she had back then was a head full of hazy dreams. The New York life she fantasized was full of parties and discos and fascinating people and phone calls from directors telling her she'd just beaten out Meryl Streep for a part.

And some of those dreams *have* come true. She has a lot of interesting friends in New York. Most of them, though, are in the same boat she is — hanging in, living three or four to an apartment, surviving on frozen pizza and diet soda, waiting for their lucky break.

And Jordan isn't the worst off. At least she *has* found work on a real stage. Actually, it was a revolving stage at the Sandy Toes Dinner Theater in the Round out on Long Island. For three weeks she had a walk-on as a file clerk in a comedy about office life called *The Water Cooler*. Unfortunately, her part came early in the first act and so she usually had to shout her lines over people clinking silverware and eating dessert and ordering coffee.

She clicks off the Walkman and puts it in her pocket, as she gets up and heads down the swaying aisle of the train car. The doors to both bathrooms are marked OCCUPIED, so she leans against the wall by the water spout, pulls a little amber plastic bottle from her jacket pocket, takes out a pill, and washes it down with a paper cup full of water. "The One-Course Lunch," is what Nell calls Dr. Don's pills. In ten minutes or so, she'll feel as though she's just had a submarine sandwich and three cups of coffee.

Finally, one of the bathroom doors opens and a large woman and two small children emerge, like clowns from one of those tiny cars in the circus. Jordan waits for them, then slips inside and shuts the door behind her.

She looks in the mirror, feeling betrayed by the florescent lights around it. The smudges under her eyes are darker than usual, and she's breaking out again. She pulls her makeup bag from her backpack and goes to work. In fifteen minutes or so, she looks more like her old self.

"Thank heavens for Cover Girl," she says aloud, giving her face in the mirror a parting pat before opening the bathroom door.

Back in her seat, she puts her Wallkman back on. Mostly, this is a defense against the old woman who has the seat next to her. When the trip started, she talked Jordan's ear off for half an hour, about her grand-children, all of whom, according to her, are astounding successes. The girls especially. The ones who aren't brain surgeons or air-plane pilots are stars in major ballet com-panies.

This was not a line of conversation Jordan was particularly comfortable with. And so she just told the woman that she was study-ing French for her new job as cultural at-taché in Paris, and this was her practice tape.

Back under the influence of Keith Jarrett's moody piano playing, she falls into the dream-like state that's the closest Dr. Don's pills ever let her get to a real nap. She drifts into think-ing about the reunion, and about seeing her oldest, closest friends. Sweet dumb Leigh. Superwoman Sue. Scooter the madman. And, of course, Graham.

Graham. At the thought of him Jordan slides into deep daydream, the same one she's been having all week, ever since she decided she *would* come to the reunion, even if she wasn't returning in glory. The dream is a replay from the highlight tape of her life — the last time she saw Graham.

Scene:
Jamesburg Country Club, fourteenth
   fairway
3 a.m.
Prom night — senior year

Off in the distance, there were changing lights from the ballroom in the clubhouse, and the bass-heavy chords of Eddie and the Losers, the local rock band hired by the senior class for their prom.

But the music and lights were dim and distant out here. On the fourteenth fairway, it was dark and quiet. Jordan reclined against a small grassy slope. She was wearing a pale peach dress and drinking champagne and raising her glass to Graham every time he slammed another ball into the black darkness.

She was watching his shoulders shift beneath the white linen of his dinner jacket as he connected with the ball, then followed through with the club. She's never known anyone who moved as easily, as gracefully as he did. She wanted to tell him, and at the same time couldn't imagine herself actually saying anything like this. And so instead she said,

"That's a pretty weird golf outfit, fella."

"Utrastyle, woman. I am simply on the cutting edge of golf fashion. You, however, are a pretty weird-looking golf groupie."

It was like this the whole year she'd gone with him. She just couldn't let him know how she really felt about him. This had something to do with having known him practically all her life from the neighborhood, having been Stampers before they were boyfriend and girlfriend. The Stampers were always either being sarcastic, or goofing around. None of them ever said anything straight on, and Jordan and Graham carried this stuff over into their romance.

But all the kidding around and never being serious was also protection for Jordan. So he wouldn't ever see her straight on. If he did, he'd see that she really did love him. She just couldn't handle that.

She was uncomfortable with love, afraid to let herself feel it. Her relationship with her parents was about one step above plant life. She was more affectionate with her brother Phil, but even with him, who she'd known all her life, she was more comfortable keeping it loose and light.

Graham was her first shot at romantic-type love. At first she thought maybe she'd be able to do it, let him inside the icy cool Jordan persona. But she got scared. It was easier to hide a bit, to always let him think she cared for him just a little less than he cared for her. Tonight, this lie would be especially helpful to her.

"Hey coach," he turned and said, "I think my strength is ebbing. I need some more training champagne."

He dropped the club, came over, and fell beside her as if he were going into a set of push-ups. And the last instant, he turned so that he landed on his side next to her.

"Oh, I am a happy guy," he said. "For sure the happiest guy at this prom. For one thing, I'm not having to dance to songs I love while they're being murdered by Eddie and the Losers. For another, I'm with the second most wonderful girl here." More Stamper talk. There was no *first* most wonderful girl. It was just a way of taking back the compliment a little.

Jordan poured some champagne into the glass and offered it to him. He looked hard into her eyes.

"Why do I have this feeling you're about to tell me something I don't want to hear?" he said.

Jordan didn't say anything.

"You've made up your mind," he said.

She nodded.

"So you want to go to New York and be a big star. So you don't want to follow me up to State and be a golfer's sweetheart. Well, I can't blame you for that. But why can't we go our own ways and still be a couple?

There'll be holidays and vacations and it's not like we'll be a million miles away from each other — "

She put her index finger over his lips.

"Don't. Don't say any more. Geographically, New York and State may not be that many miles apart, but you know that in every other way they're worlds apart. I don't know what's going to happen to me in the city, but I have to be free to go for it, whatever it is. And I won't be able to do that if I think you're somewhere — anywhere — waiting for me to eventually come back to you. No, it's got to be a clean break."

"Like in third grade, when you fell out of that tree in my backyard and fractured your arm?"

"Oh Graham, you don't forget anything, do you?" Jordan said and leaned in and kissed him. Then she pulled away and said, "Clean breaks heal fast. You'll be up at State meeting a million people. You won't take long to get beyond this. And of course, we'll always be friends."

He hopped to his feet at this, tossed the champagne glass against a nearby tree, watched it shatter into a thousand pieces, and said, "Oh Jordan, I wouldn't count on that."

And then he loped away, through the woods at the edge of the course.

Chapter 2

Graham is sound asleep in the passenger seat of his ancient Fiat. Sue's doing the driving on this last leg of the trip back from State University to Jamesburg.

She downshifts the reluctant gears of the convertible into the next curve of the old two-lane highway. Overhead, branches of maple trees are so heavy with rustling leaves that they form an arched ceiling. Sunlight filters through in tiny dapples. Birds sing wildly, as if they're doing a major production of a bird opera. June is settling in on this part of Massachusetts.

Sue loves this kind of driving — gliding the old sports car along back roads, feeling the rush of wind running through her hair, getting a little time alone with her thoughts. Which she has a lot of these days — large confusing thoughts messing up her usually orderly mind.

She knows her solitude won't last long. Graham is beginning to mutter. Which means he's about to wake up. As usual, the muttering is about golf.

"Nine iron to the green," he says now. Graham got into the state university last fall on a partial golf scholarship. He always acts like this is a joke, tells everyone he's majoring in putting, minoring in sand traps. But the amount of dream muttering he does makes Sue suspect he takes the sport more seriously than he admits. Graham never acts like he's taking *anything* seriously, so she has to guess at what's important to him.

Now he's moving around in the low, cracked leather seat, stretching his arms above his head, running a hand through his thick red hair. He just got it cut really short. The top stands up in red bristles. It's pretty punk. Sue's still not used to it. Sometimes she laughs when she first looks at him. Like now.

Even though he's still half asleep, he sees her laughing and sticks his tongue out in response, then looks around at the passing scene.

"So," he says, "you didn't total my car while I was out. You can drive without my constant supervision. Amazing."

"And we're almost there," Sue says, "maybe forty miles more. I'm getting kind of nervous."

"It *is* going to be pretty weird seeing them all again," he says, sliding a hand on the back of her neck and rubbing it. "Especially with all that's happened to us this year."

10

And he doesn't know the top item on that list, she thinks, wondering when she's going to find the perfect moment to tell him. She's been looking for it for two weeks now. Maybe this is it. She opens her mouth and tries to push words out, but nothing happens.

"The thing is," Graham goes on, "we're going to be a big surprise to them, but they're going to be a big surprise to us, too. I mean, we really don't have a clue about what any of them have been doing this past year. Jordan's in New York, but all we've gotten from her are those mysterious postcards with King Kong hanging off the Empire State Building. She's supposedly becoming a big star, but I have to say I haven't seen her in any magazines yet."

"Be nice," Sue teases.

"Oh, sweetheart," he says, leaning over and kissing her lightly behind her ear, "you know I'm not in love with Jordan anymore. I'm not even hurt about that anymore. Since I fell for you, it's like everything that came before was just trainer wheels."

Sue smiles and takes her hand off the gearshift for a moment to give his a squeeze. Never having had a boyfriend before Graham, she's sometimes overwhelmed at how much of a boyfriend he is, how attentive, how *there.* He says he's just hopelessly devoted, like in the song.

Now he's going on with his list.

"Leigh. Another mystery. She was supposed to stay in town and go to haircutting school. But when you called last week, her mom said she's up at some college in Maine. A pretty amazing fact considering how much trouble she had getting out of high school, how much trouble she had learning to tie her shoes in first grade. Remember?"

"Mmmhmm," Sue says. "And what about Scooter? All we know is he moved to California. He calls you and says he's been selling tofuburgers on an amusement pier. He calls me a month later and says he's a lifeguard at a relaxation tank."

"Don't forget that three-in-the-morning call when he sounded so wired. Babbling about how he was working at the zoo. Putting on a comedy show for the monkeys. To keep their spirits up. I think he's become a lunatic."

"He's always been a lunatic. I think living in California's just let him really run with it," Sue says. Then, "Hey. I'm going to pull off here and get us a couple of Cokes."

The Fiat's tires crunch through the gravel shoulder as she turns into the dilapidated old gas station, really just a weatherbeaten frame shack with two pumps in front. She brings the car to a stop in front of a huge new, bright-red Coke machine, which looks totally out of place here.

"The Coke Machine From Outer Space," Graham says.

The sagging screen door squeaks open and the owner — a big guy in a grease-streaked undershirt — lumbers out. Graham tries to wave him off.

"Just getting a couple of Cokes," he says, tacking on an apologetic grin.

"Kids," the guy says, clearly disgruntled at having come out for nothing. He pulls a large bandana out of his back pocket, wipes off his neck and disappears back inside.

"Is that what we are?" Graham says, hooking his thumbs in the waistband of his Levis, leaning against the machine as Sue slips two quarters in and waits for the can to come thudding through the chute. "Are we really still kids? Does that seem possible?"

"Maybe you are," Sue says, "but I'm pretty sure I've just been disqualified." She hopes Graham will pick up on the remark, and give her a way into talking about The News.

But he's far far away now, back in the past. His thoughts are triggered, not by the reunion this weekend — one year after at Jamesburg High — but by the reunion *within* the reunion — the reunion of the Stamp Club.

Scene:
Leigh Weller's front steps
Hot August afternoon
Last week of vacation before high school
*   begins*

The five of them — friends since sandbox days — were just hanging out, like they had been almost every day for the past two-and-a-half months. The three girls and Scooter were sitting on the steps.

Leigh was on the top step, scrunched over, reading a magazine called *Teen Hunks*. She was wearing an outfit that probably wouldn't get the interest of a teen hunk — old, stretched-out shorts and a T-shirt with a computer picture of her dog, Steve, on the front.

On the step below her, Sue — whose brown hair, after all these weeks junior lifeguarding at the town pool, had lightened almost to blond, then gone slightly green — was reading the instructions that came with the Golden Chestnut coloring foam kit she had just bought.

Graham was doing wheelies on his bike, mostly to impress Jordan, who was either polishing her nails and not noticing him, or pretending to polish her nails and not notice him. At fourteen, Graham had way too little experience with girls to know which.

They were talking about the jump they were about to make from incredibly boring but safe Fillmore Junior High to exciting but moderately awesome Jamesburg High.

Each of the girls had her own worry.

Leigh's worry was that nobody in high school would carry a pencil case, and she'd have to give up the one she'd had since first grade, with its ruler top and built-in sharpener.

Sue's worry was that two years wouldn't be enough to really prepare for her SATs.

Jordan's worry was that senior guys wouldn't be interested in her and the sophomore and junior guys would be too dippy.

They were passing around Leigh's older sister's Jamesburg yearbook from the year before.

"Hey," Scooter said. "Here's a trip. We can make up a club for ourselves. See. They have a group picture of every club. Like these turkeys here in sombreros — they're the Spanish Club. But the trick is we gotta think of a club nobody else will ever want to join. So it's just the five of us in the picture. That means it has to be something *really* nerdy."

"The Octopus Club," Leigh offered.

"What does the Octopus Club do?" Jordan asked.

"We raise and train octupuses," Leigh said.

"And when they ask to see these specimens of the deep — what're we going to do? Attach some hoses to your brother Ricky and paint him gray and put him in the bathtub?" Sue asked. "No, we've got to have a club with at least *some* credibility."

"A stamp club," Graham said. "All we need is a few stamps, and there's no one nerdy enough to want to join a club that collects stamps."

"Ronald Trout," Jordan said.

"No," Scooter said, "not even old Fishbreath. He might secretly collect stamps, but he wouldn't want everyone to know he collected them. No, Graham's got it. If we form

15

the Stamp Club, when they take that picture in June, we're going to be the only ones in it."

And they were. Every year. Holding among them the big fake leatherette album that only contained three stamps from Costa Rica and two from Iceland. In a way, the pictures were an in-joke. But in another way, they were really a record of a strong, complicated, five-way friendship.

And then came graduation and the club disintegrated, its members drifting off in different directions. Stamps on letters to different places.

Chapter 3

The Fiat slows as it passes the Jamesburg City Limits sign.

"Pop. 8,364," Graham says. "Looks like no one birthed or deathed while we were away."

"And they didn't take us off the count," Sue says. "I guess they knew we were coming back."

It's an old joke. No one in Jamesburg, not even old Mr. Brent, can remember when the sign said anything but Pop. 8,364.

"It really does look like nothing's changed around here," Graham says, peering around as they cruise Main Street. "See. The special at the Lunchbox Café is *still* chicken pot pie, green peas, and cherry cobbler. And look, the library window still has old Creeley's BOOKS TAKE YOU TO MANY LANDS display. The construction paper must be disintegrating by now. And look — " now he's really getting into this " — there's Kevin O'Connor out on the basketball court, still trying to make a slam dunk."

Just as Graham is saying, "Nope, nothing has changed around here," Sue turns into the Bucky Burger lot and slams on the brakes. They both hang speechless for a moment in front of the weirdest person either of them has ever seen in Jamesburg. Sitting on the back of a beat-up old Ford is a guy in black jeans and a black leather vest with no shirt underneath. He's wearing spiked wristbands, reflector shades, two gold hoops in one ear. His hair is short on top, long and combed back on the sides, with a tiny tassle of hair down the back of his neck. Most amazing of all, though, is that this visitor from another planet immediately begins waving and smiling at them.

"Hunh?" Graham says, turning to Sue for help. But by this time the guy has come over to the car, is opening Graham's door, and dragging him out with nugies on the arm and a general burst of friendly fooling around.

Sue is the first to recognize him, but can only half believe her eyes.

"Scooter?" she says tentatively.

The superpunker looks up, clearly surprised at her surprise.

"Of course," he says, letting go of Graham's arm, "who'd you think it was — Mad Max?"

"Wow," Graham says. "It *is* you. You look so strange, man."

"Oh come on," Scooter says, "I always looked strange. I just look a different kind of strange now. You look a little odd yourself.

A real lawnmower job here," he says, running a hand over the top of Graham's hair. "Sue looks the same, though. But then she was middle-aged by the time we were in fifth grade." She climbs out of the car to strangle him, but he pulls her into a hug before she can get him.

"Gee, it's *good* to see you, Scoot," she says, hugging him back. "We were just wondering what's up with you, how you've been. I gather you haven't joined the corporate world yet. This does not look like the young IBM exec image."

"No, I'm still living out in Venice. I've got a job on the pier now. I sit on this little ledge in a cage over this big vat of jello-y stuff and yell insults at people. They throw baseballs at this bull's-eye target and if they hit it, the seat gives way and I fall in. It's a job where it pays to look as freaky as possible. You get the largest number of people teed-off that way, and the more teed-off people, the more baseballs they buy. It's not bad work. Kind of creative really. You've got to be a good actor. I know I probably sound like the guy in the joke, the one who sweeps up after the elephants at the circus. When someone asks him why he doesn't quit, he says, 'What — and get out of show business?' Wow, I guess I'm kind of frothing at the mouth here, aren't I? It's just that I'm so excited to see you two. And hey — there's so much I want to talk about with you guys. But right now I've got to go. Got to visit a friend."

He jumps into his car, starts it up with a roar, then leans out the window and says, "Hey. I forgot to mention, I call myself Scott now. Scooter's dead."

And with that, the engine again roars ominously and he's off. Graham and Sue look at each other, exchanging a little unspoken communication.

A car hop comes out of the Bucky Burger stand carrying a tray.

"Hey," she says, "where's the weirdo who ordered the Double Cheesebucky, fries, and a chocolate shake?"

"The masked man just rode away, Jeanette," Graham says, recognizing her as a girl from the class behind theirs — a senior this year. "He left a silver bullet for you, though."

"Oh boy. Graham Powers. And Sue Sullivan. I forgot. This weekend's when they're letting all you old fogeys come back to school. I suppose the masked man was a mystery celebrity alum. I'm impressed," she says sarcastically, and turns back toward the restaurant.

"Who's this 'friend' he's rushing off to see?" Sue says. "We know all Scooter's friends. We *are* all Scooter's friends."

"Yeah, something strange is going on," Graham agrees.

"I don't know," Sue says. "How do you define strange when you're referring to Scooter DeLucca? I mean, we *are* talking about the Pied Piper of Jamesburg."

Scene:
The Stamp Pad
A Thursday night
Spring of high school junior year

Scooter's loft was high up in the rafters of the old Rialto Theater. He'd been living there since his father had left town for a construction job in Florida. The only furniture in this ancient cavern of a room was a mattress, a row of old maroon velvet movie seats, and Scooter's stereo.

The day he moved in, he'd painted the place purple. At night, the purple walls got bathed in the orange glow of the neon RIALTO sign hanging outside the front windows. It was a very eerie look.

Before Scooter had been in the loft even a week, the rest of the Stampers had claimed the place as the Stamp Pad — their home away from home and all-purpose hangout. By now the place was filled with Jordan's Broadway show tune records, and Sue's easel and paint table, and Graham's golf clubs, and Leigh's little old black and white tv set. Not to mention the ton of assorted sweaters and shoes and hats and empty soda cans and styrofoam Big Mac boxes. Not to mention Marco and Polo.

Marco and Polo had become residents of the Stamp Pad and official mascots of the Stamp Club one night about two weeks after Scooter had moved in. He was walking by the alley that ran alongside the theater when he heard the trash cans meowing.

Knowing that it's extremely rare for trash cans to meow, he did a little poking around and found, inside a cardboard box on top of one of the cans, two small, scared kittens. He brought them up and set out a bowl of milk, intending to keep them for the night, just until he could find a home for them. They had been there ever since.

All the Stampers had ideas about what the kittens should be named. Jordan wanted Jane and Dustin (after Jane Fonda and Dustin Hoffman, her favorite actress and actor). Graham wanted Bogie and Birdie, golf scoring terms. Sue thought Monet and Manet, after the French Impressionist painters. Leigh suggested Happy and Lucky. But Scooter overruled everyone.

"I found them, and I buy their Tender Vittles, and so I get to name them. And since I'm Italian, I'm naming them after my favorite Italian in history — Marco Polo. The gray one's Marco. The tortoiseshell guy is Polo."

Tonight, all of them were there, including the kittens, who had grown almost into cats by then. Graham and Leigh had made dinner — macaroni and cheese with tuna — and afterward everyone had agreed to play Risk with Jordan. By now she had all but won. Her eyes were bright, her cheeks flushed with victory. Jordan always won at Risk. Scooter was usually too distracted, Graham too laid-back,

Sue too cautious and sensible in her playing, Leigh too plodding and fearful. Only Jordan had the ruthlessness of the conqueror.

By now Leigh was already out of the game, and had wandered over to the windows, where she was leaning over the sill, looking dreamily down on Main Street, her lank brown hair falling around her face, her chin in her hands. Polo was walking around her feet, leaning in to brush against her legs as he passed, purring.

The others were still sprawled on the floor around the game board. Jordan was taking away Scooter's last country.

"Ah! I've got you in Western Europe, Señor Scooter. I'm afraid that wipes you out. You're done for. A broken man."

"What I really like about Jordan," Scooter said, "is what a gracious winner she is."

"I'm not a winner yet," Jordan said. "I still have to knock Graham out of Venezuela. I don't know why it is, Graham, but I especially like conquering you."

"That's interesting, because I especially hate being conquered by you."

At this, the two of them slid into matching smiles. None of the others noticed.

Leigh was off in space, daydreaming about following Main Street out of town to the highway and following the highway to the next highway and keeping on going around the world. At the moment, she was riding her bicycle through China. Leigh was full of thought lately. Inside she was often on a round-the-world excursion, or deep into some discovery about herself. She was timid about expressing this stuff, though, afraid she would blurt it out all wrong and get laughed at by the others. And so mostly she just kept it all to herself.

Sue was bent over the board, trying to figure out how she could use her pitifully small armies in Africa and Greenland to keep Jordan at bay. At the same time, between her throws of the dice, she was outlining an essay for world history. It was on Marie Curie. Also, in the margins of her thoughts, she was

a) figuring up how many more hours of baby-sitting for the horrendous Robertson children she would have to do before she could afford an electronic typewriter to do her papers on;

b) contemplating what she, as president, was going to say at the next Student Council meeting;

c) wondering what colors she should use for the background of the portrait she was doing of Jordan, and

d) estimating what the chances were of the girls' basketball team (she was star forward) beating Higbyville Monday night.

Sue was a person with an overscheduled mind. And so she had no concentration left over to notice superfluous things like the smile that passed betwen Jordan and Graham. Or the fact that Jordan had just taken Greenland from her.

Scooter didn't notice any of this either because, now that he was out of the game, he was off in a corner playing his guitar. It was an acoustic guitar, but now that he was deep into his Bruce Springsteen phase, he wanted an electric one. Until then he did what he could to emulate Bruce. That is, he didn't wash his hair and he wore jeans and white T-shirts. Of course, none of this made him look or sound anything like Springsteen.

None of the Stampers wanted to tell him this, though. They didn't want to burst his bubble. Since Scooter had been left on his own he'd been pretty down. He wrote sad songs, like "Girls Make Me Want to Hide in My Locker" and "Hang Up When She Answers." They were too tricky for the Top 40, but all the Stampers thought they were good — even Jordan who made a big point of hating rock and only listening to jazz.

Now, while she was taking over what little was left of the world, Scooter was noodling around with a new song.

"What do you think about Marie Curie?" Sue asked Jordan.

Jordan stopped, holding the dice in mid-air. "I know this is going to astonish you, Sue, but I hardly ever think about Marie Curie. I guess you could say I'm just not heavily into French scientists. Hey. It just occurred to me it's Thursday night and you're not baby-sitting at the Hendersons. What's up? I thought Thursday was sacred — Evelyn and Richard's bridge night."

"I told them I was sick and couldn't come. I've come to the conclusion that the Henderson kids are demonically possessed."

"What are your clues?" Graham asked.

"Let me just give you the latest example. Saturday night, all five of the little beasts ambushed me, tied me up with ropes from their Forest Ranger Roger tent, left me there in the family room while they all went bowling, then came back and dared me to tell Evelyn and Richard when they got home."

Graham and Jordan looked at each other, nodded, burst out laughing, and said, at the same time, "Yep. Demonic possession."

"We'll go with you this weekend," Graham said. "The five of us are bigger than the five of them. We can tie *them* up and go bowling. Hey Scooter. What's that weird little tune I hear you playing?"

Scooter twanged out a few more chords before telling.

"It's called "Pied Piper."

And then he went back over the first verse.

Yeah I'm the Pied Piper of this hopeless town.
I play my guitar and they all follow me down.
    down.
    downtown.
    fool around.
I show them a good time.

"Oooo, I like that," Leigh said, looking over her shoulder, shuffling into a little dance to it, moving over toward where Scooter was playing. He started doing the same little dance, slow-timing around the room singing and playing.

Yeah I'm the pied piper, I play all the
tunes
that get them all dancing
and out of their rooms.
away from their glooms
away from their dooms
Feeling good and dancing.

Graham was the next one persuaded by the song. He got up, taking the Risk board with him. Accidentally on purpose. All of Jordan's markers slid to the floor.

"Hey, Graham Cracker!" she wailed, using the kiddie nickname that made him crazy. "What do you think you're doing? I've almost won the whole world!"

"Okay then," Graham said, "I give it to you. I don't know what you're going to do with it, though. It's really an impossible place."

As he said this, he held out his hand to her and pulled her to her feet.

"Come on, Genghis Khan," he said. "Even conquerors have to punch out and have some fun once in a while."

And so Graham, with Jordan in tow, danced into line behind Leigh and Scooter, weaving around the room. Sue was the only one still sitting on the floor. The others weren't about to let this go on for long. They wound around back to her and circled her as they danced.

"You all know this is too silly for you," she said.

"Sue the Sensible," Graham teased. He was always telling her that she was more middle-aged than his mother. This drove her crazy.

"Come on," Jordan said, "you can count it as exercise. If you dance with us now, you can skip your aerobics tomorrow morning."

Reluctantly, mostly to get everybody off her back, Sue got up and joined the rest of them. Pretty soon, though, she was into it, into the music and the spell of the weird orange and purple light.

They all danced around the room a few times and then suddenly Scooter opened the door and slipped out, still playing and singing. Leigh hesitated for a second or two, then followed him. Graham and Jordan, still holding hands, followed without a hitch. Sue was the only one who stopped at the doorway.

"I think the city ordinance is that you have to have a permit for a parade of any kind," she called ahead to the others.

At this, Jordan turned and gave her a look that pretty much said if she didn't come along, she was an impossible turkey and they would all have to reconsider her as part of this select band of friends. It was quite a look, and instantly persuaded Sue to come along.

Down the stairs they went, past the steel doors leading to the upper balcony of the theater, past the lower balcony and the main floor, out through the lobby past an astonished line of popcorn buyers, and onto Main Street.

Everyone stopped to stare. Some of the adults shook their heads and muttered about drugs.

But the Stampers were only high on each other, and on spring, which had just hit Jamesburg this astonishingly warm night.

Scooter led them the two blocks to the fountain in front of the town courthouse. It was a small fountain, circled by a little pool, and its waters danced with the colored lights playing on them. Scooter didn't even take off his running shoes, just stepped over the stone edge and kept on playing and singing as he got in and began tromping through the water around and around the fountain. The others — even Sue was caught up in the ridiculousness of the situation by now — followed behind him, dancing and splashing.

Two grizzled old bums — Harry and Beano — who had sat on the courthouse steps for as long as anyone could remember, drinking wine from a small bottle inside a paper bag and commenting on the world, watched this spectacle for a while before offering their considered assessment.

"Lunatics," Harry decided.

"Nope," Beano contradicted. "Interplanetary visitors."

The Stampers heard this. Graham burst out laughing and collapsed into the pool, taking Jordan along with him. The other three watched their bubbles for a minute or so. The bubbles got closer and closer together, then stopped altogether just before Graham and Jordan — who had known each other since their mothers pushed them up and down Ritter Street in strollers and who no one had ever known to have the slightest romantic interest in each other — came to the surface locked in one of the juiciest kisses ever seen on the streets of Jamesburg, Massachusetts.

Chapter 4

Jordan is standing in the middle of her old bedroom at home. She's still holding onto her nylon dance duffel. She's forgotten to put it down.

"I've kept everything just the way you left it," her mother says. "I wouldn't know where to begin getting rid of all this junk anyway. I think you'd need dynamite to even make a dent."

"Yeah," Jordan says, still looking around.

"I see living in New York has made you an even livelier conversationalist," her mother says. She and Jordan haven't gotten along for years. Now she just looks at Jordan and shrugs. "I put a towel in the bathroom for you. And there's a plate of brownies down in the kitchen. It doesn't look like you've eaten anything since you left last spring."

When her mother has gone and shut the door behind her, Jordan puts down her bag. She begins moving around the room slowly, like a tourist in a museum, looking at everything. Everything is significant. And this *is* a museum — filled with relics of a girl who no longer exists. She went away to New York and never came back. Someone else did, but not this girl.

Not the girl who has an entire wallful of photos of Hall & Oates.

I haven't listened to their records in months, Jordan thinks, remembering all the nights she went to sleep thinking about what she'd wear at her fantasy wedding to Daryl Hall.

She moves across the room and looks at the Paris street scene Sue painted for her six-teenth birthday. She lifts the painting from the wall and turns it over to read the in-scription she knows is on the back.

"For Jordan — a little piece of Paris, until you can really get there, to the place of your dreams."

And suddenly Jordan can remember when Paris *was* the place of her dreams, where she and Daryl Hall would go on their honeymoon. And even though these dreams seem incred-ibly dopey now, Jordan feels sad, not for hav-ing lost them, but for having lost the inno-cent girl who could dream them.

She sinks down onto her old bed, which is lumpy with stuffed animals. She shakes her head in amazement that she could ever have had a stuffed animal collection. Or a room done completely in pink. Or ruffled curtains. Or a dresser top full of little bottles of the world's most wretched cheap colognes. Enticement. Seduction. Panther's Kiss. Voodoo Night. Had she really thought that junk was going to attract anything but large insects?

She leans back against the wall and immediately hits her head on a protruding pushpin. She turns and sees her collection of snapshots. Mostly her and Graham. At the beach. (*His nose is so sunburned.*) At the Christmas Snowball dance. (*He looks so cute in his tux.*) Kissing in a rowboat out at Carson's Lake. (*Who took that?*)

She suddenly realizes that she is crying slow silent tears. Lately, she has begun to feel that breaking off with Graham was one of her bigger mistakes. Maybe though, just maybe, it's a mistake that's reversible. Maybe this weekend will provide her with a second chance.

"Jor! . . . Jor! . . . *Jor*dan!"

At first this calling comes from a great distance, another dimension. Then, slowly, it becomes clear that it's her mother, shouting from downstairs.

"Jordan! Phone."

It's him. She just knows it.

She jumps up and runs out into the hall where the upstairs phone has sat on the floor ever since she can remember. She picks it up and can hear — on the other extension — her family rattling around and talking in the kitchen.

"Will someone please hang up down there?" she shouts over the banister, then goes back and waits. When she hears the reassuring click of privacy, she puts her mouth on the receiver and says, in her huskiest voice, more sighing the word than speaking it, "Hello?"

"Jordan?" It's a girl's voice on the other end of the line.

"Leigh?" Jordan guesses. It's been so long and the voice is a little different from the Leigh she remembers. She can't be sure.

"Yes. Hi. Did you just get in?"

"Mmhmm," Jordan says; her interest in this conversation has just dropped about thirty points.

"Me, too. I don't know if any of the others are in yet. You're the first Stamper I called."

This is surprising to Jordan. Of the five of them, she and Leigh had always had the most trouble getting along. And clearly nothing has changed. Jordan has always been impatient with Leigh's slowness, and now, mere seconds into this conversation, she feels the old exasperation welling up again. But really, isn't it just like Leigh to equate just getting in — probably from a walk down to the drugstore — to Jordan coming all the way home from New York? *She probably hasn't done anything interesting all year, just gone to that beauty school and come home and watched tv,* Jordan thinks, then feels guilty for the thought. It isn't Leigh's fault that she couldn't get into college, or didn't have any big dreams to follow like Jordan.

"So," Jordan says, making polite conversation, "how've you been? How's the haircutting thing going?"

"Oh," Leigh says, "I dropped out of that."

Predictable, Jordan thinks, in spite of her resolution to think kindly of Leigh.

"But lots of other things have been happening," Leigh rushes on in a breathless voice. "And so fast. It's exciting, but scary, too. You know?"

"Unhuh," Jordan says, although she really can't imagine anything about life in Jamesburg that would qualify as exciting or scary. But then, maybe to Leigh, who's used to life in the slow lane — life on the entrance ramp, really — maybe for her Jamesburg is a thrill a minute.

"What about New York?" Leigh asks. "Are you a big star yet? I look for your name in the magazines."

"Uh, well, it takes a little longer than just a few months," Jordan says, irritated that Leigh has zoned in on this touchy issue. "I *have* been acting, though. And I'm getting lots of good workshop experience. And I'm starting to make important connections. I'll tell you all about it when I see you. You going to the dinner tonight at Chen's?"

"Home of the Killer Egg Roll? Wouldn't miss it for the world."

Jordan's a little surprised. It's not like Leigh to make jokes. It's not even like Leigh to *get* jokes.

"Are you driving over?" Leigh asks now.

"Yeah, my mom said I could use the car."

"Mine's going out tonight. I wonder if you could pick me up?"

"Uh, sure," Jordan says.

"It starts at seven."

"Then I'll come by for you about quarter after. I don't want to be the first one there."

"Good old Jordan," Leigh says. "Always into the grand entrance."

"Yeah, well, see you in a couple of hours then," Jordan says, hanging up, nettled that Leigh has seen through her strategy.

She goes downstairs to see what's happening. Her brother Phil is eating the brownies.

"Why don't you just inhale them?" she says. "It'd be quicker."

He sticks his tongue out at her. It's covered with brownie.

Jordan likes Phil a lot, even though he's two years younger and interested in almost nothing but computers and girls. They have always had the same sense of humor, and a basic understanding of each other. Jordan figures she lucked out in the brother department.

"They're really for you," he says, pointing a half-eaten brownie at the rest of the brownies. "Mom made them as a coming home treat. She likes you better than she lets on."

"She likes me better when I'm not around," Jordan says, not taking a brownie. This is not because she doesn't want a brownie. She would kill for a brownie. She would jump from a great height onto someone walking by with one of these brownies, and grab the brownie and run. It is taking every last ounce of willpower to not eat one of these brownies. But she won't. Because brownies are the way to becoming fat, and becoming fat is not the way to get acting jobs. Except for once-in-a-century fat people parts.

So instead, she reaches into the watch pocket of her Levis and pops her emergency Dr. Don pill.

"What's that?" Phil asks.

"Vitamin," she lies.

"You look like you could use a few. I mean, if you don't mind my pointing out this fact — you do not look real terrific."

He's looking across the kitchen at her with real concern. He's not teasing, she knows.

"I'm just tired from the train," she lies again.

"You look like you're cosmically tired, kiddo," says Phil, who is not easily fooled.

By the time Jordan pulls her mother's Camaro into the Weller's drive, it's past seven-thirty. She honks, but although every light in the house seems to be on, no one comes out.

Impatiently, Jordan gets out, goes up to the door, and rings the bell. Almost immediately, the door is opened by a cute redhead in white jeans and a navy polo shirt with a green cotton sweater tied around her shoulders. She has a big smile on her face.

Jordan stands there feeling awkward. The girl looks vaguely familiar, but Jordan just can't place her. Some friend of Leigh's sister Lana? A relative, a cousin or something, visiting from out of town? What confuses Jordan even more is that all the while she's puzzling this out, the girl doesn't say anything, doesn't ask who Jordan's come to see. She just keeps standing there with that smile on her face.

Finally, in a low voice, she says, "Jordan. It's me."

"Leigh?" She can't believe it.

The girl nods.

"B-b-but how? What. . . ? Where are. . . ?" Jordan starts to crack up at her own inarticulateness. Leigh leaps in to help, giving Jordan a quick hug and talking a mile a minute.

"I'll try to fill in the blanks. The glasses are gone. I've got contacts now. The hair is a souvenir from my beautician days. The missing twenty pounds is due to the majorly terrible food at Barton College."

"What. . . ?"

"I told you a lot was happening to me these days. Come on. I'll tell you on the way to Chen's. If we're going to make a grand entrance, we probably ought to get there before everyone leaves."

Chapter 5

On the way out to Chen's, Leigh tells Jordan all about the changes she's been through this past year. Her frustration with beauty school. Her determination to get into college, even though everyone thought it was beyond her.

"I just knew it wasn't." Her jaw has a certain set to it as she says this.

Jordan looks across the front seat. Leigh really does look great. And she seems so confident and determined to succeed. And so happy. Maybe she underestimated her all along. Maybe Leigh wasn't really dumb and dull and aimless. Maybe all that glazed daydreaming she used to do behind those linty glasses was just her larvae stage, sitting in her cocoon until she burst forth as a butterfly.

And in the same time, what has Jordan accomplished, she asks herself? Last year at this time, she already *was* a butterfly. Now she feels like a moth.

She's doing the best she can to disguise this tonight, though. She spent two hours getting ready for this dinner. Washing and conditioning and blowing dry her long blond hair. Giving herself the full makeup treatment, including double color eyeshadow. Pressing her hottest outfit — black silk pants and matching shirt. Senior year she wore only black, as a kind of trademark. And so she wants to make her grand entrance tonight as a blast from the past, the return of the phantom. It's a performance for a limited audience. Although there were seventy-five kids in the class, and fifty of them will probably be there tonight, there's really only one person she wants to impress as she sails in.

She pictures him sitting at the table, talking to somebody. And then — before he even sees her — he'll sense her presence in the room. As if she's exerting a powerful magnetic field. He'll be compelled to look up and straight into her eyes. And everything will — in an instant, without either of them having to utter a word — be just as it was between them. Their love will be back in full force.

Which isn't quite how it happens. In the first place, in spite of arriving nearly an hour late, Graham is nowhere to be seen when Jordan makes her grand entrance.

The place is mobbed. On the way in, Jordan and Leigh get stopped half a dozen times by old classmates. Joe MacLeod — who's working in his dad's hardware store and has a beard now — can't believe how great Leigh looks. He doesn't comment on Jordan, which immediately throws her into a paranoid tailspin. If he didn't say anything, it must mean he thinks she looks awful.

But then Stacy Conners — who's engaged and flashing a ring with a really small diamond — comes up and asks Jordan for her autograph.

"I'm not kidding," she says, holding out a pen and a cocktail napkin. "I heard you were a big star in New York. I think I saw you on *All My Children* a couple of months ago. You were great. They dyed your hair black for the part, though."

"Oh. Yeah," Jordan says, letting Stacy go on with her mistake. She doesn't bother telling her she's never been on anything as good as a soap. She just smiles in acknowledgment of the compliment and moves on through the crowd, looking around all the time — without looking like she's looking — for Graham.

Finally, she and Leigh reach the back room.

"Jor." Leigh tugs her sleeve. "Look over there. Tell me it isn't true. Tell me that isn't Scooter."

He's sitting by himself, saving a round table in the back. He has propped up a sign — a blow-up of a two-cent stamp with magic marker letters underneath saying RESERVED FOR STAMP CLUB.

"Wow," he says when they both go over

and hug him, but the remark is clearly meant for Leigh. He can't seem to take his eyes off her.

"Wow yourself," Leigh says. "If anyone gets the prize for the most dramatic image change, it'll be you, Scooter."

"Scott," he says. "I go by Scott now."

"Is that your real name?" Jordan asks. "I thought it was really Scooter."

"Jordan," he says, "how could anyone's real name be Scooter? Can you imagine any couple in the hospital with their pride and joy, and the husband asks the wife — 'What do you want to name our little darling?' And she says, 'Well, since he'll probably wind up President of the United States, we'd better give him a serious name. What about Scooter?' No, it was just a nickname that stuck too long. When I got to California and didn't know anyone and could start all over, I thought it was a good time to drop it."

"Is this how everybody's wearing their hair in California?" Leigh asks, giving the little tail of hair at the back of Scooter's neck a playful tug.

"Uh, well, I'm not sure," he says, shyly, a little nervously. "I got this from a girl at a party one night. It was kind of a surprise in the morning." It looks like he's going to say more, but instead he just changes the subject. "Hey, you know, I've been holding this table here for years. These eggs rolls arrived around February. They've congealed back to their natural essence — cold grease. So, where've you been?" He's talking a mile a minute. He seems at a loss for something to do with his hands. First he rubs them together, as if warming them in front of a campfire. Then he shoves them in the front pockets of his flak pants. Then he runs them through his hair.

"You mean Sue and Graham aren't here yet?" Jordan asks.

Scooter shakes his head.

"I saw them at the Bucky Burger this afternoon when they were on their way into town. But they haven't shown up here yet."

"Nice they had each other to ride in with," Jordan says. "Probably the first time they've seen each other since they got up to State. I've heard that school is so big you can't find anybody or anything there. Supposedly they still have students from the seventies who can't graduate because they can't find where their last course is meeting."

"Well," Scooter says, now moving edgily from foot to foot, "I guess Sue and Graham managed to find each other just fine. True love, you know. Or didn't you?"

Jordan feels her heart drop about a foot, right into her stomach, but she recovers in time to look at Scooter nonchalantly and say, "Oh, no. I hadn't heard. What a surprise. It's really hard to imagine them as a couple, though, isn't it? But then I don't suppose it's anything very serious."

At the same moment that Jordan's heart is

dropping into her stomach, Sue's is flip-flopping around inside her. Graham has come by for her in the Fiat.

"Boy, am I starving," he says. "A good thing, too — going to New England's worst Chinese restaurant. Starving is really the only condition that prepares you to face Chen's. Merely hungry won't do."

He turns the key in the ignition and starts up the engine. She reaches over and turns it off.

He looks at her with a question mark in his eyes.

"I need to talk to you," she says, brushing her hair back off her small serious face. When she doesn't say anything right away, he waits patiently. Finally, abandoning all her smooth rehearsed lead-ins to the subject, she just says, in a barely audible voice, "I'm late."

"I know," he says, "but we'll still get there for most of the fun. All we're missing are the egg rolls and you know they're terrible."

"No. I mean I'm *late*."

He shakes his head.

"I don't understand," he says. "Late for what?"

Sue gives out a huge sigh.

"I don't know why I'm so weird. How can I be perfectly open and completely unshy about going to bed with you, but not be able to say the word 'period' in front of you?"

"Your period's late?"

She nods.

"How late?"

"Three weeks."

"Did you take one of those tests?"

"Yeah. Two days ago. It came up positive. I made an appointment with the women's health center in Boston for next week. I guess the test could be wrong. But being realistic — which as you know I always am — I think I'm probably a pregnant person."

"Oh, boy," he says, sinking back into the seat. "We should've used something. How could I have been so careless?"

"It's not all your fault. I was there, too, if you remember. Every time. Sensible Sue Sullivan throwing caution to the winds. I guess when the sensible fall in love, they really come crashing down."

"Sue —" Graham starts to say.

"Don't," she says, putting her hand gently over his mouth. "Don't say anything now. I've had three weeks to think about this. You've had about three seconds. I want you to take some time before you react. We can talk later. For now, I just want you to know. I felt like I was excluding you. I needed to let you in. It was getting lonely here."

Graham nods and leans in and kisses her softly, then says, "One thing I don't need to think about before I say anything is that I love you very much."

When Graham and Sue come through the doorway into the back room at Chen's, Sue sees Scooter hailing them and leads Graham over by the hand. Graham barely sees his old friends.

Jordan smiles at him. He stares back at her. He's a million miles away, lost in his thoughts. But Jordan interprets this differently.

He can't take his eyes off me, she thinks. *I was right. The thing with Sue was just killing time. Now he's back and he wants me more than ever. I've got to help him get away from her, though. I've got to make a move.*

Chapter 6

The Stampers are among the last of the reunion crowd left at Chen's. They've saved their fortune cookies, and now they're opening them up.

Jordan's says YOU WILL JOURNEY IN AN UNEXPECTED DIRECTION.

Scooter's says ROMANCE ON YOUR HORIZON.

Leigh's says YOU WILL BE CALLED ON TO HELP A FRIEND.

Graham's says SURPRISING NEWS FROM LOVED ONE.

Sue's says CHANGE IN PLANS ADVISED.

"Hmmm," Leigh says. "Think they'll come true?"

Graham and Sue exchange knowing glances. The others shrug.

"I know!" Leigh says. "Let's hang onto these. I'll put them in my treasure box at home, and next year we can look at them and see which came true."

A silence falls over the table. It's clearly time to leave Chen's. A waiter is vacuuming around them. Still, none of the Stampers want to call it a night just yet.

Scooter, who has been acting odd all evening — first nervous, now draped on his chair like an overcooked noodle — suggests they all go for a moonlight swim down at Miller's creek. This used to be a favorite late-night summer thing for them all to do.

"I don't know," Leigh says. "It's only June. That creek is probably still mighty cold."

"Oh come on, chicken," Scooter says. "If it's too chilly for you, you can just lie on the bank and get a moontan."

"Be sure you get the kind with moonscreen, though," Jordan adds, tossing her long blond hair.

While she's talking, Graham reaches under the table and gives Sue's hand a squeeze.

"Do you want to go?" he says in a low voice.

Sue nods.

"Sure. It's fine," she says. "I like being with the Stampers. It's like being a kid again."

By the time they all stop to pick up their swimsuits and get out to the creek, it's nearly midnight. The night is warm and windless. The sky is alive with stars. Although the creek is a popular swimming spot, it's early in the season and late at night, and so it's deserted except for the crickets and animals rustling around in the dense surrounding forest.

At the swimming spot, the creek is wide, with several large flat rocks in the middle.

"Last one in's a rotten egg!" Graham calls when they've all changed and are standing on the bank. He's wearing his old cut-offs with the pockets hanging down below the frayed edges of the pants legs. "Beat you all to the rocks!" he says as he cuts a neat jack-knife off the bank into the deep black water.

Jordan and Scooter follow right behind. Sue and Leigh hesitate a second or two, look at each other, and begin laughing.

"I don't want to go in there," Sue says. "It's probably freezing."

"My sentiments exactly," Leigh admits. "I'm nice and warm and dry right now. If I go in, eventually I'm just going to have to get out and spend half an hour getting back to this perfect state of blisshood."

"What say we just put on our beach robes and sit under a tree and talk each other's ears off?"

"*My* kind of exercise," Leigh says, as they settle down with their backs against a huge old maple.

Meanwhile the other three have reached the rocks and climbed up.

"Chicken-hearted lily-livers!" Graham shouts back across the creek at Leigh and Sue. "It's not cold at all!"

"It really isn't, is it?" Scooter says, standing next to Graham, looking scrawnier than ever in his baggy Hawaiian print trunks. He lies down and stretches out on his back on the rock's surface. "It's kind of like a nice summer afternoon. Except, of course, that it's completely dark out."

"Speak for yourself, you guys," Jordan says, shimmering in the moonlight in a pink iridescent swim suit. "I'm chilled to the bone. Can I get a little hugging action here, just for a warm-up?" She's looking at Graham as she says it, but he pretends not to understand. They stand there looking at each other for a moment that begins to grow awkward. Finally, Scooter leaps up to save the day.

"All right. All right," he says, putting his hands on Jordan's arms and rubbing briskly up and down. "It's a dirty job, but somebody's got to do it." He pulls her into a friendly hug as Graham dives back into the water.

"Gonna take a little swim, friends," he calls back over his shoulder, and begins cutting through the water with sure strokes.

"Why do I get this feeling," Jordan says, watching him go, "that he does not want to have much to do with his old girlfriend?"

"Well, I think he's pretty involved with Sue now," Scooter says. "I call them once in a while. From what I gather, it's a pretty heavy number."

Jordan seems not to hear this.

"I wonder if he's still so hurt by my rejecting him that he can't talk to me."

"Oh, I don't think that's it, Jordan," Scooter tries again.

"I'll bet that's it," Jordan says, as if they're really having a conversation.

Leigh and Sue sit next to each other, shoulder-to-shoulder. A little wind has come up, and the branches above them are gently wooshing.

Leigh's face is turned toward Sue, her mouth is a little open, her eyes wide.

"Are you sure?" she's saying.

"Pretty," Sue says, looking down at her hands.

"How far along are you?"

"Not very."

"Wow. I just don't know what to say — congratulations, or I'm sorry. I mean, how do you feel about it?"

"Confused," Sue says, pulling her terry-cloth beach robe tighter around her shoulders.

"I'll bet. Do you know what you're going to do?"

"How do you mean?" Sue says, turning to look Leigh in the eye.

"Well. There *are* options."

"Oh, I'm going to have this baby. My only questions are about how I'm going to work this into the rest of my life. I'm nineteen years old and until this I've always done everything sensibly. Now I've gone off and done about the least sensible thing imaginable. One year into college, lots more away from being the architect I want to be, eight months into my first relationship with a guy — and I'm going to have a baby. Which throws a curve into everything. What's the Sensible Sue solution to such an unsensible dilemma?"

Leigh thinks for a few minutes. Sue waits. Having known Leigh for practically all their lives, Sue is used to waiting through Leigh's thinking processes. When she comes out on the other end of them, she says, "Maybe since it's not a sensible dilemma, the sensible solution doesn't apply. Maybe you ought to forget about what you ought to do and just do what you really *want* to do."

"But what *is* that?" Sue says.

"Oh. I think *you'll* have to figure that out. I know this is complicated for you, but I really am happy that you're in love. I always wanted that to happen to you. You were always so sensible, though, I wasn't sure it ever would."

"How can you tell I'm in love?"

"Oh. I think anyone looking at you and Graham would just have to know. Are you thirsty?"

Sue blinks, trying to figure out how this question connects with the conversation. Then she remembers that Leigh often doesn't bother with connections. So she says, "Yeah, I am kind of. Why?"

"I brought along a six-pack of Tab. I can go get it out of the car."

"Fine," Sue says. "There's a couple of bags of chips in the backseat of the Fiat. Bring those along, too, will you?"

She leans back against the rough bark of

the tree and listens to the soft flapping sounds of Leigh's rubber shower sandals padding away.

Leigh gets out to the small clearing where the Stampers have parked their cars. At first she thinks she's alone and reaches through the open window of her mother's car to get the soda. Then she hears a slight creaking. It sounds like the sound of person against vinyl. She leaps back with a start and looks around. She sees, in the backseat of Scooter's old black beater, a tiny orange pinpoint glow of someone smoking.

"Scoot?" she says.

"You rang?" he says from within.

"What're you doing in there?" she says, edging over toward the car.

"What do you think?"

She sniffs.

"Well, from my limited collegiate experience, I'd say you're smoking a joint. I didn't know you smoked dope, Scooter."

"Scott."

"I forgot."

"There's a lot of things about me you don't know."

"Like that since you've been out in California, you've become a major druggie."

"That's one," he says, and leans over and throws open the door. "Come on back here and keep me company."

"Okay," Leigh says, bending down to squeeze past the folded-down front seat, into the back. "But just for a minute. I'm getting some soda and chips for me and Sue."

She settles in the opposite corner of the backseat from Scooter, pulls her feet up, and clasps her arms around her knees. Scooter takes a deep drag off the joint, then holds it out to her. She shakes her head no thanks.

He's holding his breath and so doesn't say anything right away, just stubs out the joint on the chrome trim of the open window. Finally, he exhales and says to her, "I can't get over all the changes you've been through. I guess you know you look great, Leigh. Everyone at Chen's must've told you. I myself am impressed. Even after a year of looking at California girls."

"Aw Scoot. I mean Scott. But the outside changes are really the smallest ones. Inside is where I'm completely different. It's like I keep coming around corners and surprising myself."

"I'm surprised you decided to go to college," Scooter says, putting his bare feet up on the back of the front seat. "I thought you were all set on that hair cutting deal."

"Not exactly," she says. "It was everyone else who was set on that. My parents. Mrs. Bell. I saw her half a dozen times last year and every time I told her I really wanted to go to college, but she discouraged me at every turn. My grades just weren't good enough. And it wasn't as if I'd been goofing off. She knew from my teachers that I did my work, that I really was trying. I just wasn't cutting it. And then Mom and Dad kind of got into the act. They said they didn't want me getting in over my head and then feeling bad about myself. Better to take on something I knew I could handle."

"You know," Scooter says, talking softer and more slowly than usual, "I never thought you were all that dumb."

"I'm *not* all that dumb," Leigh says. "What I am is slow. And I'm not the only one. I was watching one of the morning shows one day before I went to beauty school and they were interviewing this woman who was a slow learner. Everyone called her dumb all her life, but she knew she wasn't really. And then finally she found this teacher who believed in her and worked with her and showed her she could learn just as much as anyone else. It would just take her longer. Now she's got her Ph.D.

"And then she gave the names of some colleges that have programs for slow learners. I took them down and wrote away to Barton because it was closest. And I got in at the beginning of winter term. My folks came around right away. Mrs. Bell still has her doubts. My big fantasy is inviting her to the commencement ceremonies when I get *my* Ph.D."

Scooter chuckled.

"Old Bell. I'd go by what my fortune cookie said before I'd take her advice on life. She gave me a bunch of those aptitude tests and it came out I would make a terrific forest ranger. I mean, give me a break." He thinks for a moment, then adds, "Not that I'm doing that much better on my own guidance."

"Are you really doing a ton of drugs?" Leigh asks, reaching over and giving Scooter's spiky hair a loving scruff.

"No," he says. Then, after a long pause, "just half a ton."

Scene:
Scooter DeLucca's house
Saturday afternoon in May
Seventh grade

Leigh had been clutching the stems of her daffodils tightly all the way up the block. By the time she got to the weatherbeaten wood steps of the old DeLucca house, the bouquet had a limp, strangled look to it. She tossed it behind a shrub, embarrassed to be bringing such a crummy gift.

She felt weird bringing a gift anyway. It wasn't a party. There wasn't anything to celebrate. And because of all the millions of times she had come here before, for no reason at all except that she was Scooter's friend and this was his house, she felt doubly strange showing up with presents, like some visiting dignitary, or an afternoon caller out of a Victorian novel.

It had been a while, though, since she had just stopped by to hang out here. Since Scooter's mother had come back from the hospital the second time.

Before she got sick, Mrs. DeLucca had always been the friendliest and most open and fun of all the Stamper mothers.

Lots of times she'd just on the spur of the moment tell them they should all stay for dinner. She was making spaghetti and had a giant pot of sauce going already and what was another box of pasta? No problem.

These were great old times. All the Stampers would jump in to help out, grating cheese and cutting up stuff for a salad — Mrs. DeLucca's policy on salads was that almost anything was an okay addition except maybe ice cream — and running down to Herb's Grocery to get big bottles of soda, and fetching extra chairs from around the house, and calling their parents to tell them they were eating at the DeLucca's that night.

And somehow, the three DeLuccas — Scooter and his parents and the four extra Stampers — would all squeeze around the old kitchen table with its formica top patterned with what looked like scribbles of ball-point pens of different colors.

At first, Mr. DeLucca would look a little put upon, having all these surprise guests. But pretty soon he'd get into it. Whatever Mrs. DeLucca got into her mind, she had a way of making everybody wind up thinking it was a great idea.

Maybe it was that she was so enthusiastic about everything — her dark eyes flashing, her wide smile lighting up the room. It was just kind of contagious. Like when she wanted to know how kids were dancing these days.

Everyone just stood around looking at the floor at first, hoping she would forget the question. But she wouldn't.

"Oh come on," she taunted the Stampers, "I won't embarrass you with this. If you give a party I promise I won't come down and start bopping through the basement. Your secrets will be safe with me. I just want to know. I myself am an expert in dances of the paleolithic era. I'd be glad to show you some of these ancient tribal mating rituals in exchange for yours."

And so they got out some Police and Eurythmics and Talking Heads records and showed her how they danced. And she got out her old Shirelles and Roy Orbison and Smokey Robinson's Greatest Hits and showed them how to fast dance, and pony, and hitch hike, and stroll, which especially cracked them up.

But that was all before Mrs. DeLucca got sick and went into the hospital for the operation, and came out looking like a shell with nothing inside. It was cancer and had gone too far for anything to be done.

She went in for chemotherapy, then radiation treatments, but just got thinner and paler. The treatments made something happen to her beautiful dark brown hair and she started wearing bandanas. The brightness drifted out of her eyes, the smiles came much less often and were faint carbons of the old ones.

At first, the Stampers kept coming around, to show they were behind her in this. But they could see that even their old familiar company began to be too much for her. They wore her out more than they made her happy. And so they started hanging out at the other houses.

And then she went in the hospital again. When she came out the second time, the Stampers saw almost nothing of Scooter. After school, he went straight home to take care of her until his dad got off work.

The Stampers all knew — although none of them wanted to say it — that going easy on Scooter's mom wasn't the only reason they were staying away from the DeLucca house. They were also afraid. There was something scary about seeing someone who'd been so much alive before now slowly drifting off to this other place that was death.

But when two weeks went by without seeing Scooter except in the halls at school, Leigh decided that her fears were less important than her friendship with Scooter and his mom.

And so, without telling any of the others, she picked the fistful of daffodils from her backyard and headed over.

She rang the doorbell, but even though she could hear it going off beyond the screen door, no other sounds followed.

She rang again, was about to give up and turn back when she remembered how Mrs. DeLucca loved to spend time in her garden out back, growing tomatoes and basil for her sauces, and grapes for the wine Mr. DeLucca pressed in the basement.

She walked around back, into the yard and sure enough, Mrs. DeLucca and Scooter were out there.

It was a great spring day, with high sun and fresh breezes — perfect for starting the year's garden. Which was what Scooter was doing. He had already put in the tomato plants and staked them along the side fence. Now, along the back, he was cutting back and retying the grape vine.

Leigh had never known Scooter to help with the garden. He always acted a little embarrassed around how Italian his parents were. They had both come to this country as small children, from the same village in the south of Italy. Their families knew each other, and their traditions were important to both of them. Scooter just wished they'd be more regular. No parents on any of the tv family shows made wine in their basement.

But now here he was, trimming the vine as though he were a worker in an Italian vineyard. A few feet away, lying on a rollaway bed he'd obviously brought out for her, was Mrs. DeLucca. She looked very small under the light blanket, propped up by several pillows, watching Scooter trim a vine whose grapes she'd probably never see.

Leigh stood in the shade by the side of the house and watched the two of them and knew there wasn't much more time for Scooter's mom, and how scared they both must be.

She turned around and left. There was no place for her in this moment. And yet it was a moment for her, too. It was when she started loving Scooter.

Chapter 7

The old rattletrap alarm clock goes off under Jordan's pillow. She put it there the night before so no one in her house would get curious about why she was getting up at five-thirty on this vacation Saturday.

She is *so* sleepy. She didn't get in from swimming with the Stampers last night until nearly two.

She drops the clock to the floor and puts the pillow over her head. Sleep. She's dying for it.

But no. She absolutely *has* to get up. Graham said last night that he was going running this morning — his oldest most favorite thing to do in Jamesburg. She hadn't been able to ask him when exactly did he think he was going to start out. That would've been a little like throwing a giant net over him.

Last spring, when she and Graham were an item, they would often run together. Early morning runs through the town and out into the surrounding foothills. Through the cool morning mist and into the rising warmth of the day ahead.

That was during the time when Jordan was wearing only black around school, for dramatic effect. But for those runs, she always wore white — white shorts, and a cut-off T-shirt, and a long scarf tied around her head with streamers streaking behind her as she went.

When they first started running together, Graham had to slow down so Jordan could keep up. But pretty soon, she started getting her wind, and building her leg muscles until she was as fast as he was.

And then they sailed together, two blurs on the morning horizon. They ran hard, sweating, pushing against wind and time and themselves to go faster and faster.

They took various routes, but their favorite took them down Main Street, out past the little old schoolhouse, which was now a town landmark. Past the Sunoco station and the Long John Silver restaurant, over the railroad tracks, down the two-lane highway that ran past the old mill on the creek. Up into the hills — the hard part — and then down again and around, coming back into town through the woods beyond the cemetery.

They started slowing down about there and by the time they got to the courthouse lawn, they were cooled down and ready to drop. Which they did. Right onto the courthouse lawn. At that early hour, no one was around yet, and so they could just lie in the grass, between the flower borders, far enough apart so that, with their arms outstretched, the tips of his fingers just touched the tips of hers. Even though they often didn't say a thing during these runs or while they were resting after them, they were for Jordan a special kind of being close. She always hoped Graham felt it, too. She never asked him, though. That just wouldn't have been cool.

And so last night, watching him swim away from her at the creek, Jordan began to formulate this plan. Just let him try to resist her in this old familiar, slightly magical setting.

With this thought, she's able to pull her head out from under the pillow and get out of bed.

Boy, it's dark out, she thinks, and tries to remember the last time she's been up this early.

The night I came in from Neon Universe with Nell. We met those weird guys from New Jersey. The ones with the shaved heads. And danced until the place closed and then walked home while all the trucks were out picking up the garbage.

But that was *being* up at dawn. *Getting* up at dawn was another story. The last time she did that was probably the last time she ran with Graham. Her life is sure on a different clock now.

She stumbles, sleep-bleary, over to her old chest of drawers, still painted pink from when she was a little girl. There are even traces of old nursery rhyme decals — Little BoPeep and The Farmer in the Dell — that she never could get off the front of the drawers. She pulls open the bottom one and rummages through until she finds her old white running outfit.

She pulls on the shorts. They bag around the waist.

I guess I've lost weight in New York. I must have been a real tub of lard when I lived here, she thinks, pulling a belt through the loops and cinching it on the last notch, to hold the shorts up.

She looks down at her legs. They're not tan anymore. New York is a very indoor world. The muscles are still there, though, kept in shape by eight hours of waitressing every day. Of course the waitressing has also given her a pair of feet so beat-up she goes through a box of Band Aids and two packs of corn pads every week.

She stands in front of the mirror and runs a brush through her long blond hair. It still looks good. But the face. Without makeup, and at this unearthly hour, it looks pretty grim to her.

She's stuck for a moment. Putting on makeup to go running in the fresh morning seems pretty ridiculous. On the other hand, if she shows up to meet Graham with these dark circles under her eyes, how will she ever persuade him that she's the girl he used to love, and — deep down — still does?

And so, in the end, she hauls out her huge model's makeup sack and heads for the cruel lights of the bathroom.

It's a little after six by the time she gets out to Hobson's Shoes on Main. This is where she's decided to hang out until she sees Graham rounding the corner from Sycamore, on his way from his folks' house on Ritter.

Waiting in the doorway of Hobson's, she'll have just enough time to dash out before he sees her. If she works it right, it'll look to him like she's just out running, too. As if she still starts her day like this, too. It'll make him see how linked in spirit they still are.

It's incredibly boring waiting in the doorway of Hobson's Shoes. There's only one thing to do — look at the twenty or thirty pairs of shoes in the window. And so in five minutes — give or take four — Jordan has played out this thrilling activity. This leaves her with who knows how many more minutes just standing there waiting for Graham. Of course maybe he'll show up in just a couple of minutes.

He doesn't. It's nearly an hour later, near seven-thirty, when she spots that brush of red hair and those bright green shorts. By this time, she's no longer on her mark. She's sitting down, and almost doesn't make the leap out. She finally gets to her feet and springs into the street, and gets up enough speed in the half block or so before they run into each other to look as though she's been running awhile.

Graham smiles and waves when he sees her. Not wanting to break stride, he doesn't stop, but jogs in place as he says, "Hey Jor. You still get the old morning blood running, I see."

"Oh yeah," Jordan says, tossing her hair back over her shoulder, running in place herself. "I'm an addict. Couldn't miss a day. Besides, I really love running around this old town. I didn't want this morning to happen without me."

Graham grins.

"My sentiments exactly," he says. Then, as if he's catching himself, he pulls the smile off his face and doesn't say anything more.

"Say Graham Cracker," she says brightly, "as long as we're both hoofing around this burg, what do you say we do it together?"

When he shuffles some more, looking at his feet, she adds, "It'll keep us from running into each other. I think head-on crashes ought to be avoided, don't you?"

"Okay Jordan," he says, but not playfully. "Let's be running buddies. Just like old times."

And off they go, Graham pushing it, Jordan practically killing herself to keep up. Waitressing may be hard work, but she can see now it's not major aerobics.

"Well, what've we got here?" Graham taunts over his shoulder when she can no longer keep up. "New York making a wimp out of you? Stardom slowing you down?"

"Come on. Have a little mercy, will you?" Jordan pleads.

"Okay," he says, slowing down, "Mr. Nice Guy here. We can talk as we go. You can fill me in on all the gory details of life in the pulsing metropolis."

"Oh, it's pretty pulsing," she says, getting in stride with him, letting her arm brush his every so often, but not so often that it looks like she's doing it deliberately. He doesn't mention this, doesn't pull his arm away in horror. Maybe he likes it. Maybe he doesn't notice. It's hard for her to tell.

They're heading out of town now, off toward the old mill, a key place on the map of their past together. It's where they used to come at night with Graham's old tartan football blanket and lie down on the bank of the creek and make out.

But he doesn't mention this, or even look like he remembers it as they run past, just prods her again to tell him about her life in New York.

"Well, it's not as easy as I thought it would be, breaking onto Broadway," she says, deciding to be honest. There's no point in trying to bluff Graham. He's always been able to see through her. "I thought that because I'd played Blanche in the big Jamesburg High production of *Streetcar Named Desire,* I was ready for stardom. Well, that's not how it works. As soon as you get to New York, the first hundred people you run into are a hundred girls who played Blanche in their high school productions of *Streetcar.*"

"Gets you down to reality pretty fast," he says.

"Exactly," Jordan says, remembering how sympathetic Graham used to be to all her problems. It looks like he's *still* just as understanding!

"I just didn't know how much I still had to learn," she goes on. "I've been taking acting classes and dance classes and movement classes. . . ."

"What's the difference between dance and movement?" he asks, a little out of breath from running.

"Oh, there's a difference," she says. "If you can come up with the money — which hardly anyone can — you should also take classes in improvisation and auditioning."

"I thought auditioning was what you did to *get* the job."

"Well, it's like SAT prep courses. Courses teaching you how to take tests so you can take more courses. All of life's absurd, not just New York."

"And so?" He turns and looks at her questioningly. "Do all these lessons work? Have you gotten a real job yet? Have you acted on a real, honest-to-goodness stage?"

She looks back at him and decides it's safe to tell him all about her triumph at the Sandy Toes Dinner Theater. And she tells the story with all its flourishes, including the night some woman from the audience on her way to the ladies room walked across the stage smack in the middle of one of Jordan's two big lines. By the time she's done, Graham is in stitches and collapsed in the meadow grass by the side of the road.

"Stop. Please. You're killing me," he says.

She's laughing along with him and keeps on laughing until there are tears in her eyes. And then she's stopped laughing, but the tears keep on coming. She can't stop them. It's not that she's that sad, more that the tears have taken on a momentum of their own. This has happened a few times recently, since she started taking Dr. Don's pills. It's like they kind of turn up the volume on her emotions.

"You okay?" Graham says, getting up and putting an arm around her shoulder. This surprises her. Last night at Chen's, even when everybody else was hugging each other, he kept his distance from her. The way she interpreted this was that he was afraid if he touched her, he'd feel the old electricity. He's afraid to get involved with her again because he's afraid of getting hurt.

She takes it as a good sign, though, that

he has his arm around her now. She closes her eyes for a moment, so she can just feel him close to her.

It's just so right, she thinks. *He just has to feel it, too.*

Now that she has things back on the old track, she wants to keep them there.

"Tell me," he says, "is there something wrong? Something in New York?"

"Is there something right would be a better question," she says, sitting down on the grass. He follows and sits beside her. "Almost everything's wrong. Nothing turned out like I thought. I'm broke. I haven't had even a second call to an audition in a couple of months. I'm working two waitress jobs and living in an apartment slightly larger than a phone booth with two other girls and about two thousand roaches. They used to just be in the kitchen, but then there got to be so many they couldn't all fit, so now some are commuter roaches. They live in the living room and just go into the kitchen for meals.

"There's not even a real bathroom," she goes on. "The tub is in the kitchen, under a piece of plywood we use as a counter. We're on the fourth floor and there's no elevator. For a while, believe it or not, all this seemed kind of charming. You know, I'd lived here all my life. Small town stuff. I got to New York and everything was so different and exciting, and there was so much of it. But I have to work so much and have so little time or money, I can't really take advantage of it anyway. Most of the time, I might as well be back here in Jamesburg for all the interesting city things I do."

Graham is listening hard, nodding.

"I knew something was wrong as soon as I saw you last night at Chen's," he says. "You look all dragged out."

"I *am* all dragged out. Most nights, I get about four hours sleep. But I keep thinking if I just hang in for another month, maybe it'll happen. The Big Break. And then it doesn't and I hang in another month. I hate to quit. I went there to really go for it. But still, coming back here, getting away from that whole scene, it makes me wonder if I just ought to forget it and. . . ."

"And what?" he asks.

"I don't know. I don't really have a Plan B," she says, giving him the chance to say *I do. Come away with me.*

He passes up this opportunity, though, and says instead, "I don't know what to tell you, Jor. It's hard to know when to cut bait on something. Especially when it's something you thought you really wanted. Something you gave up a lot for."

"Yeah," she says ruefully. "I gave up plenty for this dream. I gave up you."

He doesn't say anything, just pulls some grass out of the ground and begins tearing the blades into little pieces.

"I'm sorry about that, Graham," she says. "I want you to know that. I feel rotten about letting you go. I hurt you."

"Yeah, you hurt me," he says, and starts thinking about the person who bailed him out of that hurt.

Scene:
Massachusetts State University
Student Union
Late October, freshman year

Graham looked up from his biology textbook for about the twentieth time in the past five minutes, and then snapped it shut in defeat. It was impossible to both concentrate *and* wait for someone who was probably going to show up at any minute.

Then, as if on cue, there she was. Sue. Good old Sue. Except in passing — once at registration, another time out on campus — Graham hadn't seen her since they both came up to State over a month ago. They had been put in different dorms on opposite ends of campus, and they were in different programs. Sue was in the art school, Graham in liberal arts. Then there was his golf, her basketball practices.

More than all of that, though, Graham hadn't really wanted to see Sue. She had called a couple of times, wanting to get together, but he had put her off. He was still too stung by Jordan breaking up with him. When she left for New York — and up until the last minute he'd been convinced she wouldn't really do it — it had been the first time in his life that he'd really lost anything.

Oh, he'd lost little things, of course — a

few golf tournaments, several steelie marbles when he was a kid, a pet frog named Horace — but nothing really big. And so when Jordan gave him up for a destination sign on the front of a bus, he was left not only hurt, but stunned.

He didn't want anyone to know how bad he was taking this, especially not another Stamper, and so he'd been ducking Sue these first weeks at college. But his loneliness had finally won out over his pride. His roommate was a guy from Maine who wanted to be a forest ranger. He was a solitary soul who enjoyed reading wildlife books, and had almost no need for talking.

And Graham *really* needed to talk to someone. So, after thinking it over for a couple of days, he decided to call Sue. He hated to admit his broken heart to anyone, but Sue seemed the best choice. She knew him almost as well as he knew himself. And he could trust her. He could make himself vulnerable to her without worrying that she'd ever use the information against him.

She was standing in the doorway, clutching a Sue-sized stack of books and spiral notebooks to her chest, scanning the huge, crowded Union grill. Graham stood up and waved until her smile indicated she saw him.

"Hi," he said when she got to the table. He stepped around and helped her put her books down, and then gave her a one-armed, brotherly type hug, then stepped back a little to look at her. "You look different."

"Oh," she said and blushed, "I guess I've gone a little collegiate. Got my hair cut like every other girl in my dorm."

"How do you like it in Holmes? I hear the girls there are maniacs."

"Only after midnight," she said, sliding into the booth across from him. "That's when the shaving cream fights start."

"In Gilchrist, the pandemonium is hall hockey. And they talk about bullfights being the most violent sport." He stopped himself. "Hey. Can I get you a Coke or something?"

"No, that's okay," she said, digging around in the depths of her knapsack. "I'll go up myself. I'm starving and the dinner at Holmes tonight is something unspeakable. Dorm cooking is turning me into a grill rat."

"But how can you afford eating in the grill all the time?"

"I've got a job. Weekends. In a nursing home in town. I'm an aide. It's hard, but I like helping out the old people. What about you? Are you working, or just a playboy?"

"They've got me golfing every spare minute. I thought this athletic scholarship was going to be a candy deal. But it looks like they want me to win a Master's tourney by spring or something."

"Gee, it's good to see you," Sue said, reaching across the table as she got up, ruffling Graham's hair. "You always were the cutest redhead I've ever seen."

When she came back with a bagel and

Coke, and chips, and blueberry pie à la mode, she asked him, "So. How are you doing up here? Stamper's truth."

"Not sure," he said. "Everything's so big. It took me a week just to figure out the scramble system in the cafeteria. I couldn't find the linen exchange until last week."

"Oh, I know," Sue agreed vehemently, "but at the same time, it's all so exciting here. All the films and speakers, and the mixers. The professors. Do you have Hanley for American lit? Fabulous."

"I guess I really haven't gotten into things too much yet," Graham said in a dead voice.

Sue looked at him hard, trying to see what was going on.

"Why," she said, "do I have this feeling there's a big central piece of information I'm missing here?" She paused for a moment. "Oh no. It's Jordan, isn't it?"

Graham nodded. "I just can't seem to get past her. I try. I've gone out on fix-ups both nights of every weekend I've been up here. I've been out with tall girls, short ones, fat and skinny ones. Dumb ones and one so smart I felt she was going to give me a pop quiz on the date when it was over. But I haven't found anybody who comes even remotely close to Jordan. For me, at least."

Sue took a long time phrasing what she wanted to say.

"Graham. I've known you and Jordan almost all my life — separately and as a couple. You're my closest friends. But I don't think it was the best relationship for either of you. And I think it had to end eventually. It was just a question of sooner or later. She wanted something on the surface. You need something deep and lasting. I can only speak from an objective viewpoint here. I've never been in love myself, and so I don't really understand the process. What I'm saying is that even though I think you're probably well out of the whole thing, as a true friend, I'll take care of you through your broken heart."

It was such a long and earnest speech that, when she was done with it, they first just stared at each other for a long moment, then simultaneously burst out laughing.

He came around to her side of the booth, slid in next to her, and gave her a Stamper bear hug. Usually Stamper bear hugs were hard, but brief — just to let the other person know you were really there for them. This one, though, lingered on for a while until it slid into holding each other, and at the end of it, Graham noticed for the first time how soft Sue's hair felt against his cheek.

Chapter 8

It's past ten when Leigh finally wakes up. At first, she thinks she's in her dorm room at Barton College, and swings down out of the top bunk. When her knees promptly hit the floor, she realizes she's in her old bed in her old room at home — the room she's shared for years with her kid sister Lana. Everyone's name in Leigh's family begins with L. Leigh can understand how when her parents — Larry and Lorraine — got together, they thought it was cute. But that they went on and named their kids Leigh and Lana still amazes her. In most other ways, her parents don't seem like turkeys at all.

Lana's bed is empty now, under what Leigh considers an excessive number of Matt Dillon pictures, including a giant poster of Matt on the ceiling over the bed so Lana can look into his eyes as she goes to sleep.

If Lana's already up, it must be pretty late. Leigh finds her clock radio under her swim suit and beach robe, which she'd tossed on the floor in the dark the night before when she'd come in from her nonswim down at the creek. The clock's digital numbers read 10:37.

She's a little disappointed. She wanted to have breakfast with her family this first morning back from school. But by now her parents are probably already closer to lunch, and Lana will already have had something revoltingly healthy — a banana and seaweed shake or something. Actually, the fact that Lana eats this kind of stuff all the time isn't nearly so sickening to Leigh as the fact that she talks about it all the time. Lana believes it makes her a better person, and wants to let everyone know.

Leigh sits on the edge of the bed for a moment, rubbing her bruised knees, then goes looking for some shorts and a T-shirt. Today's the reunion picnic at Perry's farm, and the morning is coming up hot. Outside, the ultragreen smell of fresh cut grass is filling the air as Roy Wilbur next door buzzes back and forth with a power mower beneath Leigh's window.

Leigh digs through her bureau. She finds her old favorite navy blue shorts and puts them on in front of the mirror. They bag around the waist. She keeps forgetting she's lost weight. She also forgets that her hair is now curly instead of straight.

It's mostly the way other people respond to her that makes her aware she's giving off a new image. Up at Barton, she has a lot of new friends. Many of them come to her with their problems. Her roommate Andrea calls their dorm room "The Confessional," and told Leigh once, "You're just so good with emotions. You should think about going into psychology."

And now Leigh *is* thinking about it. Funny that no one in Jamesburg — not her friends or family or teachers — ever told her anything like this, though. She doesn't think they were trying to keep her down. But she can see now that they all made up their minds early that Leigh was nice, but a little dumb. So don't tell her the tricky jokes or expect her to come up with the brilliant comeback. And, having decided this, none of them ever bothered to change their minds.

The really interesting thing Leigh's been noticing up at Barton, though, is how much smarter she is when she's with people who don't assume she's dumb.

Downstairs, everyone *is* done with breakfast. The Mr. Coffee is still half full, though, and so she pours herself a mug, then slugs it full of cream and sugar. Just the way she likes it.

"Caffeine. Dairy products. Refined sugar," Lana says, suddenly there in the doorway, a copy of a Matt Dillon magazine dangling from one hand. "Why don't you just throw in a little arsenic and be done with it?"

"How can there be enough stuff about Matt

Dillon to fill a whole magazine?" Leigh says. "Do they have articles like 'Matt Works on Cure for Cancer' or 'Matt's Opinions on Nuclear Disarmament'?"

Lana pulls a banana off the bunch sitting on the counter, then turns and leaves. She and Leigh never dignify each other's insults by responding to them. They just counter with insults of their own. It's an old way they have of talking to each other, and isn't really as nasty as it sounds. For some reason, both of them have trouble being directly nice to each other. And so they throw fake punches. Like those wrestlers on tv who are always pretending they're trying to kill each other, then after the show probably go out together for a few beers.

Leigh takes her mug of coffee and goes through the sliding glass doors off the back of the kitchen, out onto the patio where her parents are sitting in lawn chairs, watching an old Bette Davis movie on the little black and white tv they've set up on the picnic table.

Her parents are old movie freaks. They even drive all the way into Boston if something really good or rare is showing. Once they spent a whole weekend there for a Chaplin festival.

"Dark Victory?" Leigh asks, pulling up a chair herself. Having been around her parents all her life, by now she knows a lot of these pictures.

"Mmmhmm," her mother nods, crying

softly into a Kleenex she's just pulled from the box sitting ready on the table. She rates these movies by how much crying they make her do, and this one's a six-Kleenex picture.

"Hi sweetheart," Leigh's father says, ruffling her hair. This stops him. He turns to look at her. "I keep forgetting you've got this new look. Are you sure you're really my daughter and not some imposter after my estate? Just a second," he says, putting a silencing hand on Leigh's shoulder, even though she hasn't said anything. "Here's the part where Bette's sneaking through the medical files and finding out she's only got six months to live."

There's nothing to do but settle in and watch the rest of the movie with them. By the time it's over, all three of them are sobbing and pulling Kleenexes out of the community box. Lana slides open the glass door and pokes her head out and says, "Give me a break."

And disappears back inside.

Leigh's father dismisses her with a wave of his hand.

"Some," he says, "are just not true believers. We've missed your presence around the old tube, kiddo," he says to Leigh, switching off the set. "But I gather you've found true happiness up there."

"True," she says.

"You're getting something out of this whatever program?"

"Decelerated," Leigh says. "Yeah. It gives me time to get hold on one thing before we move onto something else."

"What kind of things?" her mother says.

"Well, this term I took natural science, Victorian lit, Italian, and abnormal psych."

"But if you don't want to be a scientist or a Victorian or an Italian or abnormal, what's the point?" her father says.

"*Dad*," Leigh groans.

"Come on, Flea," he says, using her childhood nickname, "you know I'm teasing. Still, I wonder about you giving up something solid like the hair school for something like this. I mean, when I was young I was interested in philosophy, but I knew I wasn't going to be able to support a family being a philosopher, and so I got into business school. Plus with you, honey, well, I've just always thought you were better in the concrete than in the abstract."

"I wasn't in the concrete at the Almar College of Cosmetology, I was in the cement. Up to my neck. Can't you see that?"

"Now sweetie," her mother says in her calming tone of voice, "your father and I just want what's best for you."

"I don't think that's exactly true," Leigh says. "I think you want what *you* think is best for me. You don't want me to get hurt failing, so you don't want me to try where I might fail. I appreciate your protection, but I think you've got to let me try to fly a little. So maybe I'll fall and bump myself. Big deal.

If I don't try, though, I'll always be grounded. Now if you'll excuse me, I've got an important picnic to go to."

"This for the reunion?"

"Yeah," Leigh says, getting up, the backs of her legs sticking to the webbing of the lawn chair — the day is really getting hot — "Everyone's bringing something out to old Mr. Perry's farm. It's completely uncoordinated, so the picnic'll probably turn out to be forty-five plates of brownies and three pieces of chicken. I'll bring that half a pie in the fridge, if it's okay. I've got to tear now. The Stampers are meeting at the courthouse at twelve-thirty."

She goes inside, then pops back out on the patio.

"I forgot, can I borrow the car?"

"As long as you're taking the pie, you might as well take the car, too," her father says. He's always saying things like this, which are kind of cryptic and off-beat. Leigh mostly finds her father an interesting person. He's just a little hard to explain to friends.

When she pulls up in one of the diagonal parking spaces in front of the courthouse, Graham and Sue and Jordan are already there, sitting on the grass. That is, Graham and Sue are sitting on the grass, holding hands, and Jordan is lying flat out in tanning position, next to them in shorts and a halter top. It occurs to Leigh for the first time all weekend (and that it took her this long to realize it makes her think she may be getting better but she's probably not getting any faster) that Jordan is back after Graham. Talk about terrible timing. She clearly doesn't know about the impending arrival of the littlest Stamper. Leigh makes a mental note to talk with her as soon as she can find an appropriate moment.

"Hi friends," Leigh says as she gets out of the car. "What's happening?"

"Oh, we're just dehydrating here on the lawn, letting the mayonnaise in the potato salad go bad," Graham says. He's just grousing because he doesn't like being out in the sun. With his fair, freckly skin he burns fast. Already, he has his nose covered with a white coat of zinc oxide. "Now that you're here, we only have to wait for Scooter — I mean *Scott.*"

"Yeah, where is he?" Jordan says drowsily, as if this conversation is bringing her back to planet Earth.

"You know," Sue says, "I'm not even sure where he's staying here in town. Does anyone know?"

No one does. Then, after thinking for a couple of minutes, Leigh says, "I think I know. Why don't you all go on out to the farm? Leave a note here in case he comes by. If I find him, I'll bring him out with me." She slides back into her father's car and roars off.

She doesn't have far to drive. Just a block down Main Street. She pulls up to the curb in front of the Rialto. The letters on the old marquee say CLOSED FOR REMODELING, but everyone in town knows that Mr. Silesky just couldn't make a go of the huge old movie house with its constant repairs and enormous heating bills. Plus most people go out to the minitheaters at the mall now. And so the Rialto sign no longer bathes Main Street in its eerie orange glow. This makes Leigh sad. It's another little indication that the town she has known all her life is changing into another place — a slight stranger to her instead of an old friend.

She goes around to the side door of the theater. She's pretty sure she'll find it open, and sure enough, it gives way against her light push.

She walks through the old musty lobby, which still smells like popcorn oil, and up the stairway with its soiled, worn-thin carpeting.

On the balcony landing, next to the doors to the restrooms, is a third, unmarked door. This, too, pushes open easily. Beyond it is a narrower staircase of concrete steps. She takes them up the last flight.

At the top is the abandoned site of the Stamp Pad. She looks around. Sunlight is streaming in through the high front windows, showing up the heavy veil of dust in the air.

It's really strange coming up here after all this time. The place is so full of memories. Off on an easel by the windows is the portrait Sue started painting of Graham, then gave up on because Graham couldn't sit still long enough for her to catch anything of him.

And then on the wall, there's Scooter's huge Bruce Springsteen poster. And running the length of the room, Graham's green felt putting carpet, with the overturned water glass at the end to catch the golf balls he spent hours lining up and tapping across the room. The little rubber water bowls marked "Marco" and "Polo" are dried up now. When Scooter left for California, Graham's family took Marco, Sue's folks took Polo.

Then Leigh winces to see the stacks of her own magazines on the real lives of the soap stars. She is aware she has a nerve making fun of Lana about her Matt Dillon obsession.

"Oh boy," she says aloud, walking over and picking up, off the back of the row of old movie seats, the satin dress that Jordan had worn as Blanche DuBois in *Streetcar Named Desire*.

"That was really some night, wasn't it?" It's Scooter. He has come out of the bedroom silently, while Leigh has been looking the old place over. "I mean, we were so knocked out. Remember?"

"Mmmhmm," Leigh says, nodding.

"We thought Jordan was a true star that night. A megastar. A nova. We thought her future was already written in lights." He pauses. "And look at her now."

"Look at all of us now," Leigh says. "None of us is quite where we expected to be a year ago."

"Graham and Sue," Scooter counters. "They're the same."

"They're going to have a baby."

"Oh boy. I guess they're not quite the same then. Oh boy."

"You said that before."

"It's just a large piece of information. It's taking me a while to absorb it. You're full of surprises this morning. Like finding me here, for starters."

"I figured you were weird about something and hiding out here."

"Well, where am I going to go besides here? It's really my only home in Jamesburg now. Some whole other family lives in our old house now. They've painted it this peachy color and put these really terrible stone deer out on the lawn. I couldn't just go there and say, 'Hi, I'm Scooter. I used to live here. Can I spend the night up in my old room?' Oh no. Can you imagine what they've done with my room? I don't even want to think about it.

"So anyway, you can see how I couldn't go back there. The Stamp Pad was really the only home I had left here. And so last night I drove over to the Rialto, expecting to see the old orange sign. I just spun out when I saw the place was closed down. I had to trick the side door open — did I ever tell you about my brief stint as a cat burglar in California? It was pretty creepy coming up those stairs. But once I got in here, everything was pretty much the way we left it. It was kind of a nostalgic night here with my thoughts and my memories. I didn't expect to see anyone else here. I'm surprised you figured me out."

"I know you pretty well, Scoot. Probably better than you realize. You never knew how much attention I was paying all along."

"Yeah, we all kind of underestimated you, Leigh."

"You especially," she says. They are only standing a few feet apart in the shadows between the huge slanting streaks of sunlight. And so it's easy for Leigh to surprise herself by closing the gap, putting a hand on his bony shoulder, and kissing him.

"Oh boy," he says.

"That seems to be today's password."

"Well, you keep surprising me, so I keep saying oh boy."

"Well, you shouldn't be surprised," Leigh says, pulling back to look at him seriously. "You should wake up and smell the coffee. Weird as you are, and weirder as you've gotten out there in California, I've loved you for a long long time, and I'm not going to stop now, just when I can finally tell you."

"Oh —"

"Scoot. If you say 'Oh boy,' I'll have to slug you. Why don't you just get your guitar and come with me to the picnic? We'll liven it up a little."

Chapter 9

By the time Leigh and Scooter get out to the big pasture behind Perry's farm, the class reunion picnic is in full-swing. More than fifty kids from their class, plus the friends and dates and, in a few cases, new husbands and wives they've brought along with them.

Picnic tables and blankets are scattered all around. A softball and a volleyball game are in progress, and a few kids are already into their swim suits and splashing around in Perry's small lake.

It's past noon. The sun is high and hot, the long green grass of the pasture is patterned with bright yellow dandelions, and blue and magenta wild flowers. Fat bees are buzzing around the blossoms. It's a very picnicky kind of day.

Along the white wood fence is a line-up of folding tables holding platters of fried chicken and roast beef and country ham. Big earthenware bowls of potato salad and macaroni salad and tuna salad, cole slaw and baked beans. A large-size box of Wheaties. (Whenever anyone tries to organize anything at Jamesburg High, there is always at least one person who gets the instructions totally wrong.) Baskets of fresh-baked rolls. Plates of deviled eggs. Layer cakes and cherry pies. A freezer of homemade peach ice cream. And, at the end of the line, a big washtub full of ice cubes and old-fashioned lemonade, squeezed from fresh lemons.

"Boy," Leigh says, looking sorrowfully down at the foil-covered, slightly squooshed pie plate she's holding. "This sure makes my half a frozen pie look pretty pitiful."

"You?" Scooter moans. "*I'm* standing here with a six-pack of Dr. Pepper."

Both of them look up to see Graham bounding across the pasture toward them. He's wearing a white golf visor, his hair sticking out the top like a bright red scrub brush.

Leigh and Scooter look at each other, getting precisely the same idea at the same time. They turn and set down the stuff they've brought, and pick up the best-looking items on the table. By the time Graham gets to them, Leigh is holding a huge platter of still-warm fried chicken, Scooter a heavily-frosted chocolate cake.

"Wow," Graham says when he gets up to them. He nods, impressed. "You guys really did a job for this."

"Oh, it's nothing, really," Leigh says. "I

come from a long line of fried chicken makers. Colonel Sanders got his recipe from my family."

"Yeah, yeah," Graham says. "And Betty Crocker ripped off everything she knows from Scooter."

"Not exactly," Scooter says, pretending to be offended, "but I did spend a few months out on the Coast working as a pastry chef in a fancy French restaurant — Le Grand Blague. Megastars like Travolta and Cher used to come in all the time for my *gateau au chocolat*."

"What's it mean — Le Grand Blague?" Leigh asks Scooter when Graham has gone off to find Sue.

"The Big Joke," Scooter says with a grin.

Meanwhile:

Graham finds Sue sitting on top of a picnic table, talking with the Malone twins — Mary Ann and Margaret Mary. They were all on Jamesburg High's girls' basketball team together. Both sisters are six feet tall and amazingly identical, even for twins. When Margaret Mary gets the braces off her teeth, there won't be any way to tell the two of them apart.

"Am I interrupting important girl talk?" Graham says, sitting down behind Sue and putting his arms around her, resting his chin on her shoulder.

"We were just figuring out how we could've

won that semifinals game against Maple-
ville," Sue says.

"We should've slaughtered the twerps,"
Mary Ann says.

"Massacred 'em," Margaret Mary says. For
sweet-looking girls with glasses and soft
voices, the Malone sisters are killers on the
court.

"Uh," Graham says tentatively, "I wonder
if I could steal my girlfriend away for a little
while."

"Guys," Mary Ann says disgustedly. "No
offense, Graham, but boys were really the
ruination of a great team. When Cindy Fred-
ericks started going with Jeff Galati, there
went our best forward. And then Rachel
Levin went goony over Steve Lambert, and
the whole season was down the tubes."

"You mean getting boyfriends made them
quit the team?" Graham shakes his head.

"Not exactly," Margaret Mary says. "But
it took away their energy. Their minds
weren't always where they were supposed to
be — on basketball."

Graham and Sue exchange a look, and Sue
says, "Well, I hope you won't think me
traitorous for going off for a walk with this
male being, but I did promise him I would.
Before the picnic. So I'm not really being a
traitor."

"You *will* be back and play a little softball,
won't you?" Mary Ann asks.

"Wild horses couldn't keep me away," Sue

says, hopping down off the table, giving Graham's visor a playful tug down over his eyes. "Well, maybe *enough* wild horses."

Mr. Perry's farm is one of the biggest in this part of Massachusetts. The pasture land covers hill after rolling hill, bordered here and there by wild woods and planted orchards. It's into one of the apple orchards that Graham and Sue wander off.

The trees are just beginning to bear the small green fruit that will eventually be this fall's apple crop. The branches spreading overhead give the orchard an airy, but still sheltered atmosphere that's somewhere between outdoors and indoors.

"I love orchards," Graham says. "They're so peaceful. They ought to put some in the center of big cities, so people could just stop in the middle of all the craziness and sit under an apple tree."

"It's just nice in general being back in Jamesburg."

"Yeah," he says, draping an arm over her shoulder as they walk. "It was cozy in my old room last night. You know, I've had that room since I was born, and I don't think I've ever taken anything out of there, just added stuff. So my whole life's on those walls and shelves, really. I was looking through a lot of that old stuff last night when I couldn't sleep. I guess I was saying farewell to my youth. And so today I'm ready to say hello to adulthood."

"What exactly are you talking about?" Sue asks, stopping, turning to look at him.

"I've decided to marry you," he says, his voice full of grim resolution.

"What do you mean, you've decided to marry me?"

"Well, I think it's the mature and right thing to do."

"That's interesting," Sue says, walking over to a low hanging branch and picking off a cluster of leaves. "But I must have heard you wrong. You must have said you've decided to *ask* me to marry you."

"Oh, uh, oh," Graham stammers. "Of course that's what I meant. Honey, I mean, will you? Will you marry me?"

"Thanks anyway," Sue says, "but no."

Jordan is sitting with Scooter on the grass by the volleyball game. They're cheering on Leigh, who's in the thick of the play.

"Vicious game," Jordan says, nibbling on a carrot stick.

"You can't really live on that stuff, can you?" Scooter says, looking down at the paper plate on Jordan's lap. It's full of more carrot sticks, and celery stalks and green onions. "I mean, don't you eventually start to grow white fur and long ears?"

"Yeah, but I'm going to be a *skinny* rabbit," Jordan says, still watching the game. "As long as I take my magic pills."

"Let me see these magic pills," Scooter says. "You got any with you?"

"Always," Jordan says and pulls one out of her shorts pocket.

Scooter takes it and nods.

"Rippers," he says and pops the pill into his mouth.

"Scooter!" Jordan says. "What do you think you're doing? You're already the skinniest person I know."

"Dexedrine isn't just good for aspiring actresses, Jordan. It's also nice for boys from California who were up too late last night and want to get a little rush to push them into the picnic spirit."

"Scooter! You're a druggie!"

"Do you think you could say that a little louder, Jordan? I think there might've been a few people who didn't hear."

"Sorry," Jordan says, lowering her voice. "Now tell me all about it. Don't spare me any details. I've heard what it's like in California — the drugs, the degradation."

"Jordan," Scooter says, "this is my life we're talking about, not a *Dynasty* episode."

"Oh. Sorry, Scooter."

"Scott."

"Scott. So, come on," she says, pinching him around his skinny ribs, "tell me what you've been up to. Have you really been leading a wild life?"

"Well, the rock scene's not exactly a monastery."

"What rock scene? You're a big rock star now and I just didn't hear about it?"

"I didn't say I was a star, just that I was

in the scene. I do bodyguarding." He flexes the muscles in his arms, small biceps and triceps. "For the Stones. Springsteen. The big boys. Whenever they're in town. It's interesting stuff. I can handle the pressure and I sort of enjoy the danger. And I like hanging out with the majors. They're really basically nice guys. Springsteen's even helping me out with my guitar a little."

"Scooter. Scott. You. A bodyguard. You've got to be kidding."

"Jordan. I am heavily trained in the martial arts now. These hands," he says, stretching them out toward her, "are registered with the L.A. police as deadly weapons."

"Oh *Scooter*," Jordan says, remembering a day long, long ago.

Scene:
Playground, Wilke Elementary School
Late Thursday afternoon, mid-January
Fifth grade
Jordan came bounding out the double front doors of school, plaid coat flying open, long scarf trailing behind her as she flew.

She was in a big hurry. She'd been kept after school for detention. An hour of sitting still in absolute silence under the unflagging gaze of Mrs. Caramangio. Punishment for talking and giggling with Stacy Redland all through math.

Now she was worried that detention would make her so late coming home that she'd get punished there, too. And so she was trying to make the half mile from school to her house as fast as she could — like a fireman, dressing as she went.

The weather was against her, though — blustering winds and walls of white, the second huge snowstorm to hit Jamesburg that week. She felt like her clothes were being undone from her before she could really get them on. She had just managed to get her coat buttoned when a tricky slip of wind came up and blew her knit cap out of her hand.

She ran across the playground after it, chasing it finally around the corner of the main building, into the passageway between it and the annex building. There, sheltered from the elements — and from the prying eyes of any teachers who might still be around — some poor little kid was getting beaten up by a much bigger one. The larger boy was throwing hard punches into the midsection of the little kid, who was trying to protect himself by doubling over. His collar was turned up against the cold, and his hat was one of those kind with a bill and ear flaps, which were down. And so it took Jordan a few seconds to see that it was not just some poor hapless little guy getting trounced, it was Scooter.

Then she recognized the other boy as Paul Cecil, a seventh grader nobody liked much. He was fat and surly and sarcastic. His father was plant manager over at the paper company and Paul acted like this put him way higher on the social scale than the other kids at school. Jordan had only seen him around — in the halls and out on the playground — where he mostly kept to himself. Sometimes, though, the other older boys would gang up and give him a hard time.

She didn't know what this fight was about between him and Scooter, but she guessed that underneath it was Paul Cecil wanting to get back at all the big guys by taking on a little one he was sure he could beat up.

These thoughts ran through her mind fast as electric current. She had to act fast or Scooter was going to be in deep trouble. And so, with absolutely no plan of attack, she just dropped her books, lunged toward the two of them, and began throwing punches at every soft spot she could find on Paul Cecil. His stomach. His back. His round cheeks. She even gave him a couple of swift kicks in the shins.

"Take that, you big blubbery jerk!" she shouted at him as she flailed away.

He was stunned. At first he didn't know where the punches were coming from, then he saw they were being handed out by a girl, and he grew even more confused. He couldn't hit back. He knew he'd never live it down if he started hitting a girl on the playground. So all he could do was stand there dumbly, letting her throw her inept punches at him while Scooter got out of the way.

She was so angry that she kept on punching for a while after there was any reason to. It was Scooter tugging on the sleeve of her coat that brought her back to her senses.

"Come on, Jordan," he said in a muted voice. He was holding his bloody nose with a big red-stained handkerchief. "Give him a break."

This drew Paul's attention back to Scooter. His eyes narrowed to little beads as he spat out the words, "Gotta have a girl do your fighting for you, eh DeLucca?"

At this, Jordan went a little insane. She grabbed Paul Cecil by the collar of his ski jacket and pulled his face up close to hers.

She was tall for her age and strong and she said menacingly, "You ever say anything about this to anyone and you'll be sorry. Maybe not right away, maybe not tomorrow, or even next week, but sometime when you're least expecting it. Some night you'll turn a corner or open a door or go into a basement. And something *very* bad will happen. Something so horrible you can't even imagine it."

She let go of his collar with a little shove, took Scooter by the hand, and walked off the playground.

When the two of them got a couple of blocks away, out of Paul's sight, they both cracked up.

"I couldn't believe that last bit," Scooter said.

"I know," Jordan said. "I sounded like the Godfather. Where'd I even come up with that stuff?"

"I don't know, but I think it worked," Scooter said, dabbing at his nose, looking at the handkerchief to see if the bleeding had stopped. "He really looked like he believed you. Cecil may be big and rich, but he's not too smart. I don't think he'll be trying to rip off any of my prize baseball cards anymore."

"Baseball cards! That's what I was risking my life and limb over! Scooter, I'll kill you myself," she said, making a playful grab at the lapels of *his* jacket.

She got into a fair amount of trouble at home, for being late, and for having lost her scarf in the scuffle. (She didn't tell her mother about the scuffle part.) But by a couple of days later, she had completely forgotten the incident. And so she was surprised, walking home the next week, when she came upon a small group of guys on their bikes. They were listening to Scooter. His back was to Jordan so he didn't see her coming.

What she heard him say as she walked up was, "Yeah, I pretty much totaled the slob. He's big, but all show and no go. And although I may be a small guy, these hands," he said, holding them out karate-style, "are lethal weapons."

Chapter 10

Even though Graham is not particularly interested in standing on the rocky bottom of Perry's shallow lake, he wants to get Sue to talk with him, and so is, at the moment, up to his chest in icy water.

"This lake is about twenty degrees colder than the creek last night," he says. "Why didn't you want to go swimming *then*, when it was sane?"

"I wanted to see your skin get nice and blue," Sue says, "like it is now. It goes so well with your red hair. Hey. How come I'm not going anywhere? I'm paddling, but I haven't moved anywhere in the past fifteen minutes."

"Because I'm holding onto the edge of your raft here. I'm trying — if you've noticed — to have a little conversation with you."

"No," Sue says, expressionless behind dark aviator sunglasses, "you want to have a *particular* conversation with me. You want to persuade me to your point of view. But at the moment, I am unpersuadable. I'd be glad to have a little conversation with you. I always enjoy talking with you. I have for years. But certain subjects are not of interest to me at the moment."

"Like . . . ?" he says, swimming along side-stroke while he pulls her raft along, parallel to the shore, but away from the beach crowded with reunion picnickers.

"Oh, like marriage."

"Okay, it's a deal. Let's talk about something completely different. Let's talk about . . . say . . . well, let's talk about bouquets."

"Bouquets?" Sue says.

"Yeah, like what kind of bouquet you want me to get you for our wedding."

Sue's fast. Graham doesn't have a chance of getting away before she leaps off the raft and dunks him.

High in the branches of a huge old maple in the middle of Perry's pasture, Leigh and Jordan — tree sitters from the earliest years of their friendship — are straddling the same branch, sharing the same Pepsi, scanning the crowd below.

"Oooh, look," Leigh says. "There's Will Travers. Couldn't you just die, he's such a hunk. He goes to Harvard now, you know. It's like college has made him even better-looking."

"It's probably made him more conceited, too," Jordan says. "I went out with him a few times when we were juniors, remember? We went over to his house once when his folks weren't home. He had a picture of himself up in his room."

"So what?" Leigh says. "So do I. So do lots of people, I'd imagine."

"An eight-by-ten framed portrait next to their bed?"

"Oh," Leigh says, and starts giggling so hard she spits out a mouthful of Pepsi. Below them, Jenny Dillard reaches up and says to Mary Ann Malone, "I think it's starting to rain."

Above, Leigh and Jordan hold their hands over each other's mouths so no one below will hear them laughing.

"I heard Jenny married Ed Farmer," Leigh says to Jordan in a low voice.

"Who's he?"

"You know, the guy who works at the Amoco station? The one who no matter what you say, he just says 'okey dokey'?"

"No! Not him!" Jordan bursts out. "Oh, can you imagine? She says 'Honey do you want meat loaf for dinner?' and he says 'Okey dokey'?"

"Well, he must have secret charms. She married him, after all, and now it looks like she's pregnant."

"Oh Leigh, it's hard to imagine, isn't it? Some of these kids married, having babies. I still feel a million miles away from that." She stops and grows thoughtful. "Not that I wouldn't be more ready if the right person came along. *Or came back.*"

Leigh feels awkward. She doesn't know

what to say. She knows Jordan is going way out on a fantasy limb about getting Graham back. Still, telling her about the baby seems a pretty drastic way to bring her down to reality. She decides to take a halfway step.

"You know, Jor, I don't think you're seeing the situation real clearly. You broke up with Graham. You went to New York. He and Sue fell in love. Now they're together. You can't come back and rewrite a year's worth of history and disrupt the lives of three people just to suit your convenience."

Jordan gives Leigh a look of total incomprehension.

"Why not?" she says.

On impulse, Leigh says, "Jordan, why not come up to Maine this summer?"

"Maine?" Jordan says with surprise.

"You know, sunshine, fresh air. All that."

Jordan smiles. "Not for me."

Scooter and Graham are standing in the high grass of the outfield in the middle of a softball game slowed down by the hot sun and the big lunch everyone has eaten.

"Oh oh," Scooter says, lifting his reflector shades off the bridge of his nose. "Terror at the plate. Your girlfriend's up to bat."

"Oh, don't worry," Graham says. "She'll whiff it." Then, just to infuriate Sue, he makes an elaborate production out of sitting down in the grass and yawning. "It's time for the outfield to take a nice break."

"I wouldn't do that if I were you," Scooter

says. "I can't quite make out her expression, but she looks to me pretty much like a bull that's just had a red cape waved in front of it."

And Sue *is* crouched over the plate with a determined expression and stance. But when Albert Donnelley, class math whiz and really terrible pitcher, lobs the first ball squarely over the plate, Sue uncoils like a sprung jack-in-the-box and misses the ball by a mile and a half.

"Hoooo haaaa!" Graham yells, then rolls around in the grass to show just how hilarious he finds her batting form.

"You are playing with fire," Scooter tells him.

And sure enough, Albert's next easy pitch doesn't get by her. Sue smacks it long and hard and straight at Graham, who gets to his feet just in time to watch it sail past his shoulder.

Scooter's on the run for it, too, but Graham — looking straight up into the sun as he goes — doesn't see him, and the two collide a few feet to the side of where the ball hits the ground and rolls off into the pasture. The two guys sit stunned while Sue ostentatiously walks around the bases, as if she's out taking an afternoon stroll. When Scooter and Graham finally disentangle themselves from one another, they look over to see Sue tipping her baseball cap to them.

"Thanks, fellas," she says.

From there, things go back to boring in the

outfield, and Scooter and Graham just fall into talking with each other.

"Scooter . . ." Graham says.

"Scott."

"Sorry. Hell, tell me something exciting, or I'll fall asleep out here. What's going on with you out there in California? You got a girlfriend? A surfer girl?"

"No, actually I'm seeing Linda Ronstadt."

"Yeah," Graham says. "Come on. Tell me what's *really* happening."

"I'm really going out with Linda Ronstadt. I know it's probably hard for you to believe, but it's true. And it's not all a bed of roses. There are problems. She's twice my age, for one thing. Plus we have to have a security man on most of our dates. That's a hassle. But I try to be a sport about it."

"Scott," Graham says. "You know you are my oldest friend and I love you like a brother, so please pardon my skepticism when I ask you why Linda Ronstadt would go out with a skinny unemployed kid like you."

"Haven't you heard? Governors and rock stars and celebrities are out in California. The newest social status symbol is skinny unemployed kids. Really, before Linda, Olivia Newton-John was after me. I told her blondes weren't my type, why didn't she find some nice guy and get married. So she did."

By now the game has fizzled out. The last of the batters has drifted off, along with most of the infield. Graham notices that he and Scooter are nearly the only ones left.

"Yeah, Scott," he says, walking backwards toward the picnic, "that's real interesting. I'm just going to get some lemonade."

"Wait," Scooter says. "I'll come along. I'll tell you how I got Christie Brinkley off my back by fixing her up with Billy Joel."

Jordan — who has been standing and staring at a huge, beckoning, lattice crust cherry pie — turns to see Graham ladling himself a paper cup full of lemonade from the washtub. He looks up just as she looks over and their eyes lock. Neither of them says anything for a moment, then Graham breaks the silence.

"Hi, Jordan."

"Hiya, Graham," she says, putting on her coolest facade.

"Are you developing a meaningful relationship with that pie?" he teases.

"I can resist anything. Except cherry pie."

"So go ahead," he says, coming over and cutting her a largish piece and handing it to her on a sagging paper plate. "You can afford to give in to temptation every once in a while. Believe me, Jor, if there's one girl at this picnic who doesn't have to worry about her bod, it's you."

He pours himself another cup of lemonade and bolts it down before running off in the direction of the barnyard.

He still thinks I'm great-looking, Jordan thinks. *And he's trying to tell me he's still attracted.* She smiles to herself, and begins plotting out a strategy for tonight at the dance.

* * *

Scooter and Sue — a mismatched pair, he in baggy cut-offs and an old T-shirt that hangs from his bony frame, she fashion-coordinated in powder blue blouse, walking shorts, and tennis shoes — are lying up in the soft, cushiony hayloft of Mr. Perry's barn, retreating together for a while from the hyperactivity of the picnic, looking down through the open loading doors onto a barnyard full of pecking chickens.

"So what's Mr. Mystery been doing this past year?" Sue asks, pulling off her tennis shoes so she can wiggle her toes in the fresh-mown hay. "Wild partying? Disco madness?"

At first Scooter doesn't say anything. Finally, he clears his throat and says, "Not exactly, Sue. You see, I've joined the followers of Yin Yang, the holy guru from Nepal. Now I travel in his wisdom. I've removed myself from the outer world, and live with other followers in an ashram."

Sue's eyes are huge with astonishment. "What's an ashram?"

"Oh, it's sort of a spiritual community. We live simply. We give Yin most of our money. With the rest, we buy brown rice and goat's milk. We wear muslin robes. Sleep on straw mats. We pray seventeen times a day."

"Seventeen?!"

"You just have to schedule a little tighter."

"Isn't that haircut a little punk for an ashram?" she says, her voice shaded with skepticism.

"Oh, Yin's a pretty hip guru. He allows us to find our own oneness with the center of our beingtude."

"Hunh?"

"But enough about me," Scooter says, ducking further interrogation. "I hear you're about to become eligible for Mother's Day cards."

"Leigh told you?" Clearly she's a little taken aback that he knows.

"Yeah. She knew the word was safe with me. You happy or sad or what?"

"I'm not sure. I haven't really had time to get beyond astonished. You know — can this really be happening to me?"

"You two'll be great parents. You'll be my favorite old married couple. I'll be Uncle Scott and drop by for cook-outs in your backyard."

"Wait," she says, putting a hand on his arm. "Stop this fantasy before it goes any farther. I am *not* marrying Graham because of this."

"Why not?"

"Because it's a terrible reason to get married. We hadn't said one word about marriage until this happened. Now all of a sudden, it's assumed. And the implication is that he's doing me a big favor. I love Graham, but I don't need him to marry me. I've done everything else in life by myself, and I can do this!"

"Whoa!" Scooter says. "Nobody here said you couldn't. Believe me, Sue, you're talking to someone who once saw you baby-sit the five Henderson kids in the afternoon and live to play a regional tournament basketball game the same night. So if you tell me you're faster than a speeding bullet, and can leap tall buildings at a single bound, I believe you. Hey," he says and pauses, "is that an enormous red-headed chicken down there in the barnyard, or could that be my oldest friend and the father of your imminent child?"

"But not my future husband," Sue says, waving down to Graham.

"Come on up," Scooter shouts, "so we can stop talking about you."

When Graham has climbed the ladder into the loft and tumbled into the hay between Scooter and Sue, he asks, "So what were you two saying about me? How handsome I am? Or what a great golfer?"

"Just that it'd be a cold day in heck before she'd ever marry you," Scooter says. He promised his mother before she died that he'd never swear. He takes the promise very seriously, and it gives his conversation some odd quirks.

"Oh she did, did she?" Graham says, leaning down on an elbow next to Sue, tickling the end of her nose with a long piece of straw he's picked up. "That's because she hasn't heard my offer. I'm about to make her one she can't refuse."

Chapter 11

After Graham drops Sue off to get ready for the big Reunion Dance tonight, he pulls his Fiat into his parents' driveway, four doors down from hers.

His father is sitting on the front lawn, reading a thick book he has open flat on the grass. Next to him is an odd assortment of five or six golf clubs, some so old they have wooden shafts.

His dad looks up and Graham slaps his forehead to show him he realizes he's forgotten their golf lesson.

"Hop in, Dad," he says, throwing the passenger door open. "There's still plenty of daylight left. We can get in a fast nine holes."

Graham has never met anyone he thinks is as interesting as his father. He thinks of him as sort of a Renaissance Guy. You'd never know this from his job, which is pretty regular and boring. He's manager of the Sunshine Garden Center out on County Line Road. But in his spare time, he has so many other interests Graham can't keep track of them all.

"What book're you on now?" Graham asks, as his father tosses the clubs in the boot and gathers his lanky frame into the passenger seat.

"*Remembrance of Things Past* by Marcel Proust. Slow going." He's been on a program for several years now. He's working through a list of the world's greatest books.

Golf is a more recent interest. When Graham got his scholarship, his father decided to take up the game, too — "so we'll have something to talk about." He's turning out to be a really terrible golfer, but he's good-natured about it, and Graham likes the time they spend together out on the course, even if it is painful to see his father hack up about three or four feet of fairway every time they go out.

The thing Graham's father likes best about golfing is that he gets to wear really ridiculous clothes. Today he has on pants printed with lollipops in various colors and a blue shirt with pink ducks all over it.

"You've been over at the K-Mart 75% off rack again, I see," Graham says.

"I thought I was being conservative. The duck shirt came in green and orange, too, but I passed that one up."

There's hardly anyone around when they get to the public course, and so they tee off right away. That is, Graham tees off right away and his father whiffs the ball three times, then knocks it off the tee with his back swing, then finally tops it about three feet onto the fairway.

"You've been practicing, I see," Graham says.

"Don't be sarcastic with your elders," his father says. "Especially if they're as dangerous when holding a golf club as I am. Besides, you know I'm only doing this so we can have a virile outdoor setting for our man-to-man talks and male bonding experiences. See, now that I've teed off, this is the part where I turn to you and ask what's new in your life lately."

"Oh boy," Graham says. "You couldn't know, but that's the tricky question of the week. Maybe of the year. Maybe of my lifetime."

"Troubles with your studies? With Sue?" his dad says, trying to give him a start.

"Well, we, well uh, we're — that is, me and Sue — well really just Sue, I guess — we're going to have a baby."

His father, who's been standing at the bottom of the tee, taking aim for his second shot, hits it straight on, for a perfect 200-yard drive. He turns around and looks at Graham in astonishment.

"I don't know which shocks me more — *your* news or *my* drive. Come on. Let's quit while I'm ahead and sit over there by the putting green and talk about my new hobby."

"What's that?"

"Well, it looks like I'm going to have to take up knitting."

Sitting together on an old park bench, Graham maps out his plans to his father.

"She won't even talk about getting married. I think she doesn't want to wind up a student wife. You know, with both of us trying to get through school, and her taking care of the baby on top of it all. So I've decided to offer quitting school and getting a job, taking care of her and the kid."

His father thinks for a minute, then says, "Why don't you make the offer the other way around?"

"What do you mean?" Graham says.

"Sue's the most goal-oriented person I've ever known. I know she's hell-bent on becoming an architect. So instead of offering to be a macho bring-home-the-bacon husband, why not offer to stay home for a while and be a diaper changer while she goes to school? You can still develop your golf. Work on becoming the best."

Graham considers this, and nods.

"A house-husband? I could, couldn't I? I can golf, too. You're right. Why didn't I think of this?" He throws an arm around his father's shoulders. "You know, it's a little embarrassing when your father always has more up-to-date ideas than yours. And you're not even the slightest bit bent out of shape about the baby. Of course I don't know why I thought you would be."

"I don't know. I might be if I didn't like the idea of you and Sue together so much. She's the girl I had in mind for you all along, you know. I was beginning to think it would never happen. But then it did, didn't it? I still don't know how you finally figured out what *I* knew all along — that you two are made for each other."

"Oh," Graham says, "I was pretty dumb about it. I didn't see it coming until it practically ran me over." He smiles, thinking of the moment when he finally knew.

Scene:
Massachusetts State University Film
*   Society*
Saturday night
Early December, freshman year

Sue watched from the wings as the lights went up in the auditorium. Everyone was still applauding the film that had just ended — *A Piñata for Miguel.* Standing next to Sue was the film's director — José Hernandez. As president of the Film Society, she was about to introduce the director and lead a question and answer session. This kind of thing was easy for her. After so many years of heading panels and chairing meetings and leading assemblies, being a public person was a breeze.

Much harder was being a *person* person. She had much less experience in that area. Tonight, for instance, fielding questions from the audience and even doing a little rough interpreting with her minimal Spanish — all that was the easy part. The hard part was scanning the crowd the whole time, trying to see if Graham was there, worrying that if he was, he thought the film was dumb and was sorry he came.

She had called in the middle of the week to invite him, then immediately felt stupid for doing it. Then felt stupid for feeling stupid. Why was she all of a sudden caring so much what Graham thought of her? She'd only known him for about a hundred years. He had seen her when she had pink eye and was there the day she'd flunked her first driver's license test by turning left from the right lane, through a red light.

All she knew was that suddenly she had started getting all wobbly inside around him, sometimes just thinking about him. At first she thought it might be some hormonal disruption she was going through. But it was too late for puberty, so it had to be something else. But what?

There he was! She finally spotted him, way in the back, under the shadow of the balcony. Was he alone, or with someone? On one side of him was a large bald man, a professor probably. It just didn't seem likely that Graham, who was as close to a nonstudent as a student could be, would have a faculty buddy. On his other side was a thin girl with long dark hair. From this distance, she looked pretty. Maybe up close she had bad skin, or missing teeth. Maybe she wasn't even with him.

But of course she was. And of course she was gorgeous.

"Sue," Graham said, introducing them afterward, at the reception in the big hall next to the auditorium, "Hillary Stafford. Hillary's from Boston. She's a film freak, so I brought her along."

Sue didn't think Hillary looked like she could possibly be an *anything* freak. She was *so* proper — her hair nearly down to her waist (probably brushed a hundred strokes every night). Her outfit a simple wool skirt and matching cashmere sweater, both in a muted forest green. Her makeup just a light blush and mascara. As Graham introduced them, Hillary held out a limp hand and briefly shook Sue's with an air of mild distaste, as if it were a dead fish.

"Pleased to meet you. Graham told me you're great childhood friends."

Sue thought they were *still* great friends, but didn't say anything, just asked how Hillary liked the film.

"Oh, Hernandez is one of my absolute favorites. When I was at Cannes last year with my parents, they had a tribute to him and I got to see a lot of his early work. I especially like *Secret of the Sarapé*."

"Oh, I've heard of that," Sue said lamely, wishing that as president of the Film Society she could say she had actually seen the movie. "We're talking about doing a Hernandez festival here. Maybe in the spring."

"Oh, that would be extremely interesting.

You really should do a combination of his films and Olga Gomez's."

"Who's she?" Sue said.

Hillary looked at Sue as if she'd said, "Who's Mick Jagger?"

"His *wife*, dear. She's the most important woman director in their country. Both their films have the same neo-realist existential ethos, don't you think? Oh, I forgot, you haven't seen any of her work."

Hillary looked around quickly, as if she was embarrassed for Sue. Or maybe she was looking around for someone more interesting in the crowd. Apparently she didn't find anybody, as she soon turned back and asked Graham, "G. Could you fetch me some punch and a few of those cookies over there?" She nodded toward the card table where refreshments were being served.

"Sure," Graham said. "Sue? You want anything?"

"Uh, no, that's okay." She was too distracted by Hillary. How did this strange new person already have a nickname for Graham? And *G. Give me a break*, she thought.

When Graham had gone, Hillary turned to Sue. "I must say I'm getting quite interested in your old playmate."

"He's a special person," Sue said.

"Well, I don't know if I'd go that far," Hillary said with a little chuckle. "But he's got definite possibilities. With a little work, he might do. The golf is a good thing. You can make more contacts on the course than you

119

can in most board rooms. But he'll have to get out of liberal arts and into business school. He'll be happier there anyway. Guys like G. need direction. Left on their own, they're all at sea."

"I don't think he's at sea at all," Sue said, indignant on Graham's behalf. "He's just on his own track. Graham isn't on anyone else's plan or schedule or wavelength."

Hillary looked at Sue as though she were a particularly annoying fly buzzing around.

"Yes, of course. He's a real free spirit. That's nice. It's just that now it's time to grow up."

Then Hillary asked if Sue would introduce her to José Hernandez, who was short and wore an embroidered vest under his suit jacket and had a goatee. He seemed to Sue very nice and not at all self-important like she had expected a big international film director would be. She took Hillary over and waited until he had finished talking with Gary Bell, the Film Society's treasurer, who was a film fanatic, and had seen every movie José Hernandez had ever made. Gary had probably seen José Hernandez's *home* movies.

Still, Gary's enthusiasm for José Hernandez looked like disinterest compared to Hillary's. She practically fell into a swoon. She was acting like someone who wanted a part in his next picture. Maybe she did. At any rate, all this fawning was done in rapid Spanish, so Sue quickly lost track of the conversation.

Suddenly, as she waited for Hillary, Graham was behind her. He slipped a paper plate of cookies around in front of her.

"Un petit snack pour mademoiselle?" he said. Graham was flunking French and so liked to hack around with it as a kind of joke on himself. "I see my date has deserted me for a film director. Can't say as I blame her. She's interesting, isn't she?"

Sort of the way a hooded cobra is interesting, Sue thought. What she said, though, was, "Well, I've certainly never met anyone quite like her before."

"That's the great thing about going to a big school like this. You meet so many different kinds of people. When we lived in Jamesburg, everybody was so much alike. You didn't get the whole panorama of human experience like you do here. Like Hillary. She's different from girls I've met before. Very career-oriented. Like you."

"Not like me," Sue said. She'd be polite, but politeness went just so far. If it meant letting herself get compared to Hillary Stafford, she'd have to be impolite. This threw Graham off. There had been an uncertain tone in his voice all through his little speech on the great spectrum of types here and what a winning example Hillary was, and now that Sue had stopped him in his tracks, he didn't seem to know where to go. He didn't ask what Sue meant, he didn't ask if she liked Hillary. He knew the answers to these questions. He and Sue had known each other so long that they could often talk without speaking. Words would just be redundant. Now — when he looked hard into her eyes and saw what she was thinking — was one of those moments.

On the one hand, Sue was glad to see the old Stamper eye-to-eye truth exchange was still in working order. On the other hand, she hoped showing Graham how little she thought of Hillary wouldn't make him mad. Maybe he was crazy about the twerp. There wasn't much to go on. Almost as soon as José Hernandez was able to get away from Hillary, she was back and wanting to leave. She took three cookies off the paper plate, slipped them in her pocket, and said to Graham, linking her arm through his, "Treats for a good boy on the way home. G. *will* take Hillary home now, won't he?"

I may have to throw up, Sue thought, but just gave as much of a smile as she could muster in the face of this romantic little scene.

Graham seemed embarrassed, but didn't make a move to untangle his arm from Hillary's. And he just nodded in response to her wanting to leave.

"Thanks for inviting us," he said to Sue.

Sue didn't remember asking *them*, but she said, "Oh, I'm glad you enjoyed it."

"I'll be calling you," Hillary said. "I think I might like to join this little club you've got here. I think I could provide some interesting input."

Save us, Sue thought, rolling her eyes heavenward toward the gods of film.

There was still a small crowd around the punch bowl, and another cluster around José Hernandez. It was half an hour before everyone dispersed, leaving Sue and Gary Bell to clean up and straighten out the hall.

"I'll fold up these chairs and clean up the programs and stuff," he said to her.

"I'll rinse out the punch bowl down in the ladies room," she told him.

Fifteen minutes later, she was coming out of the john, tired from a long day of classes followed by this long night of organizing, holding a dripping punch bowl under her arm, pushing her short hair back off her face with a wet hand. The hall lights had been turned off—super-efficient Gary, she guessed—and so at first she didn't see Graham. He was waiting outside the doorway to the meeting hall.

"Boo," he said softly. "Did I scare you?"

"What're you doing back here?" she said, trying to sound casual. "Forget your scarf or something?"

"No," he said, grinning, "I didn't *forget* anything. I just remembered how much I like you. I guess Hillary just pointed up — by way of contrast — what a spectacular person you are."

"What about all the wonderful diversity of this mega-university? I mean, Hillary's just a start. You haven't even gotten to the really different girls. What about the exchange students from other countries?" She couldn't resist teasing him. "I mean, I'm from Jamesburg where we're all boringly the same."

"You're from Jamesburg? Me, too! What a coincidence. That should give us a lot in common. For instance," he said, taking the punch bowl out of her arms and putting himself in them, "right now, being from Jamesburg, I'd like to kiss you. Since you're from Jamesburg, too, you probably feel the same."

Sue was so astonished that she couldn't find words. In the first place, she was surprised that Graham felt this way about her. She'd pretty much convinced herself it was a one-way fantasy. Added to this was her lack of kissing experience. Aside from a few games of Spin the Bottle in junior high, and a date last term with the brother of a girl on her hall — a football player who had done something smashy and boring with his lips against her lips — Sue really had never been kissed. Graham's version was nothing like the football player's. It was real soft and went on a long time, and was really a bunch of little kisses rather than one long one. When they stopped, she felt flushed and flustered, and had trouble getting air.

"Suddenly I've got a million questions," she said. "Why me? Why now?"

She was about to go on, but he stopped her with another kiss.

Chapter 12

By the time Graham and his father are
through with their nine holes (Graham, 36;
Graham's father, 102), it's misting. By dusk
the mist has turned to drizzle, by dark the
drizzle has turned to solid rain, and by the
time of the big Reunion Dance, the rains have
tumbled into a full-blown storm.

Scooter and Leigh pull up in front of Jordan's house on their way to the dance.

"I already look like I've been through a
whole long rowdy night, and nothing's even
started yet," Leigh says, looking gloomily at
her dress, which is damp and limp, and her
shoes, from which the pink dye is running
into a little puddle around her feet. "Plus,
now that I've got this ridiculous red hair, I
look like a lunatic!" She starts to cry.

"I like your red hair," Scooter says, pulling
a handkerchief from the back pocket of his
jeans. Everyone in the class decided to come
to the Reunion Dance in the same outfits they
wore to the prom last year. Scooter had worn

a white tux jacket, a black shirt, and old beat-up jeans. Now with his hair all punk and his double earrings, he looks even weirder than he did on prom night. Leigh has to laugh.

"You know, Scott. One of the weirder things about you is how in some ways you're so totally unweird. Traditional. Old-fashioned even. I mean, how impossibly gentlemanly and continental of you to pull a white linen handkerchief out of your jeans pocket."

"Sometimes I think I belong in another time. Like back when there were knights. I would've been a great knight. I'm really very chivalrous. The problem is no one cares about chivalry nowadays. At least not California girls."

"You don't have a girlfriend out there?" Leigh says. "I won't have to wrest you out of anyone's clutches?"

"Just a few groupies," Scooter says.

"You know, you're safe enough to cut the lies and clowning with me, Scott."

"Scooter."

"I thought you were changing it," Leigh says, confused.

"I don't think it's going to work. I don't think I'll ever be able to get people to take me seriously enough. I think I'm going to be a ninety-year-old Scooter."

"Not true," Leigh says, putting her arm around his bony shoulder. "You just have to give everybody time to adjust. I'm already doing it. I have to think first, but pretty soon it'll just come naturally."

"I *can* talk to you, Leigh. That's always been true, even when we were little."

"So then. Talk to me now. I want to know how you've *really* been since I last saw you. I've heard a lot of rumors this weekend, but I don't believe any of them — especially since I suspect most of them were started by you."

He laughs.

"You've really got my number, Leigh. Okay, I'll tell you the short sad saga of Scooter DeLucca in sunny California. I work driving a delivery truck for a grocery store. I have about three friends — two of them are the other delivery guys, the third is the girl who has the room above me in the house where I live. It's a boarding house. Most nights I grab a sandwich on the way home and stay up in my room listening to records. Sometimes Sherri — she's the girl upstairs — she and I go out to a movie. She's not a girlfriend. She's insane about some guy in the Merchant Marine. Mostly I don't even see her. Mostly I just hang out by myself, thinking what a neat place southern California is, how much fun everyone else is having there. And then I wonder how I can be so depressed in the middle of all this fun. And then I get depressed about being depressed. One night I almost jumped off the pier at Santa Monica. The only reason I didn't was that I figured it wasn't enough of a drop, that I'd probably only break a toe, or something that'd make me look like a dope in the emergency room. That was the low point of the past year for me. There weren't any high points."

"So you're not really a bodyguard, or in a religious cult, or Linda Ronstadt's boyfriend?"

"I see I've been talked about."

"Isn't that what you wanted?" Leigh says. "What about the drugs?"

"That part's a little true. Most of the time I don't feel I'm in sync with everyone else. I'm too slow, or too wired. So I smoke a joint, or take a litle speed. You know. To get me on the right track."

"We don't really have to have the talk where I tell you all this is not terrific for your mental health, do I? That marijuana, unlike Wheaties, is not the breakfast of champions?"

"Don't worry, Mother Leigh. I'm too broke to be a major degenerate."

"I still don't like it," she says.

"There's probably a lot about me you wouldn't like now. You're remembering cute little Scooter tricycling down the sidewalk. He was such a sweet little guy. I wonder whatever became of him?"

"He grew up and became Scott and got sad for a while, then let Leigh take him by the hand and make him happy again."

He leans over and puts his arms around her and pulls himself close to her, pressing his ear to her heart.

"Do you really think it could be that easy?" he says, so softly she can barely hear him.

"No," Leigh says, "but I think I can help. And I'd really like to. It's a way for me to get to be close to you."

"*You guys!!!*" someone shouts over the noise of the storm. It's Jordan. She has come out on her front porch in her pale peach prom dress — the dress that marked the end of her period wearing only black. Her makeup and hair are done to perfection, she looks as beautiful as she did on prom night, the one night of her life when she truly felt like a star. "I've been ready for ages," she shouts, "and now Phil tells me you've just been sitting in the driveway for twenty minutes."

"So come on!" Scooter shouts back, laughing. "Let's get going! The dance awaits!"

"But how am I going to get through this rain without winding up looking like a drowned rat?"

"Well," Scooter shouts. "We could dig a tunnel, but that'd probably take a little too long. Putting up an awning'd be too expensive. I think you're just going to have to make a run for it. Have you got an umbrella?"

"Yes, but it's so little. See?" She holds up something ruffly, like a parasol.

"Okay," Scooter says. "Open it up. I'll come out with my big umbrella and give you backup protection. I can't guarantee the results, though. Leigh and I tried the same maneuver and we're both about the consistency of kitchen sponges."

"Well, let's give it a try anyway. We can't wait here all night. People will be waiting for us at the dance."

Both Leigh and Scooter know that by "people" she means Graham.

Scooter leaps out of the car, umbrella in hand, and dashes up the steps of her front porch, taking Jordan by the elbow. He bows from the waist with a flourish of his hand.

"Sir Scott at your service, fair maiden. Your coach awaits."

They're about halfway to the car when disaster strikes. A huge gust of rain-soaked wind comes up. Jordan's little umbrella goes into total collapse under the pressure. Scooter's is pulled inside out, leaving them completely at the mercy of the elements. Which are merciless. By the time they get to the car and inside it, both of them are drenched clear through. It's one of those moments so awful there's nothing to do but laugh at it.

"What are we going to do?" Jordan wails through the tears of laughter mixed with rain in her eyes.

"Proceed onward!" Scooter says, starting up the old Ford. "We'll set the style tonight — here comes the Wet Look!"

"Just stay away from me, both of you," Leigh teases, edging exaggeratedly over toward her door. "I'm just beginning to get near damp. You could set me back hours in my drying out process."

"I wonder if everyone at the dance'll be as soaked as we are," Scooter says.

"Not Graham," Jordan says softly, to no one in particular, and sighs. "The Golden Boy'll find a way to show up perfectly dry and perfectly gorgeous."

Chapter 13

Most of the kids at the dance have been drenched by the storm. Everyone's taking it as a large joke. The girls are wringing out the hems of their floor-length dresses. Everyone's taking off their water-logged shoes and dancing barefoot.

Eddie and the Losers are back on the bandstand.

"Probably haven't had a gig since the prom," Scooter says. His opinion of Eddie and the Losers has always been consistent. "They are still the worst band in America," he says. "And I'm only putting that qualifier on it because I've never been to any other countries."

Everybody's dancing to them, though. Rick Mann and Jennifer Willis are, as usual, the stars on the dance floor. Since graduation last year, they've opened a dance studio on Elm.

Howard Snyder and Eunice Parcells are, as usual, the oddest couple on the floor. Eunice towers over Howard by about six inches, and outweighs him by about fifty pounds. They are clearly crazy about each other, though, and Eunice has her hand perfectly positioned on Howard's shoulder as they dance, to show off the miniscule diamond engagement ring he's given her.

They dance under swooshing multicolored lights and a rotating ball of mirror facets. The gym is decorated with pink Kleenex carnations and crepe paper streamers, with bunches of plastic grapes hanging on the nets of the basketball hoops. Which is to say that — as usual — the gym still looks, and smells, a little too much like the gym.

"We should've had this dance out at the country club, like the prom," Leigh says.

"I heard nobody wanted to pay the rent," Jordan says. "The gym — whatever you might say about its general pittiness and utter lack of glamor — is free."

"Yeah," Leigh conceded glumly, "but still. Just once I'd like to dance on a floor that doesn't have court markings."

"You mean Barton College doesn't have a grand ballroom?" Jordan teases. "I'm astonished."

"I know Dunbar, Maine, doesn't have the bright lights of New York," Leigh says, "but I really love it up there. I'm going to spend the summer there, too. There's this wilderness outfitter. They rent canoes for river trips. People take them downstream, then the canoes get picked up and brought back up. I'm going to be a picker-upper. Pay's not great, but I like being out in the woods. It clears my mind."

"I used to love camping," Jordan says wistfully. "My folks used to take me and Phil all the time. We caught our own fish and grilled them at night. Slept under the stars. It was fun. Boy, I haven't thought about that in a long time. Hey," she says, as if coming back down to earth and looking around, "where're Graham and Sue? It looks like everyone's here except them."

Out behind the school, in the back row of the asphalt parking lot, sitting inside the old Fiat, listening to the rain drum on the canvas convertible top, Graham waits for Sue to say something.

He has laid out his new plan in detail. She nodded all through his explanation of what he thought they should do, but hasn't said anything in response yet.

"If you're taking care of the baby," she says finally, "and I'm at school full-time, where's the money going to come from to live on?"

"I talked with my dad. He says he'll help. I think your folks will still put you through school, won't they? I mean, they were going to do that anyway. We could both work part-time. Lots of kids do that to get through. Neither of us are big spenders. We don't need much. We can make it. And we can make it together better than alone. I'm sorry I put it so stupidly before, but you have to see my heart's in the right place." With his index finger, he touches first his own heart, then hers.

"Oh, Graham," Sue says.

He waits for more, but there doesn't seem to be any.

"Honey," he presses on, "you've got to talk to me about this. It's not just your problem. It's *ours*. You're so fiercely independent you think doing it on your own is always the best way. You're afraid that letting me in means leaning on me, that it'll be a sign of your weakness. But it won't. In this case, the two of us together will be joining forces, doubling our strength."

Sue shakes her head.

"It's just that I've always had this big plan for my life, and now suddenly it's all out of whack by tossing in a forced marriage. If I do this by myself — and I know I can — it leaves our relationship free to go whatever way it was going to go on its own."

"Sue," Graham says, shoving in the clutch pedal with his foot and running the dead gears through their sequence, "I admit the timing's not great, but I love you for life. I've made a point of never being serious about anything. I guess nothing ever seemed worth getting serious *about*. Until you.

"Look. Sooner or later we would have wanted to have a kid together. I thought we'd have school and romance, then marriage, then buying a house and putting a grill and a patio in the backyard, and *then* having a baby. So, the order got mixed up a little. The baby happened before the patio. Big deal. We can handle that. And we can handle it better together. I'm not saying you couldn't do it alone. I'm just asking you to let me share this experience with you. You getting pregnant was about us loving each other. Having and raising the baby should be, too."

She turns to him and brushes her hand lightly over his hair. "You're real persuasive."

"Does that mean you'll plight me thy troth?"

"What?" she says and starts laughing.

"That's what my brother had to say in his marriage vows — I plight thee my troth. Come on." He reaches over and starts tickling her. "How can you deny me that?"

She grabs his hands and holds them still.

"Let me think about all this. Not for long. Just tonight. I just need to process everything."

"Sure," he says. "Can we sit out here while you process, though? Or do we really have to go in there, and dance to Eddie and the Losers?"

She looks down at herself in her yellow linen prom dress with its small lace collar.

"Boy, do I feel stupid in this dress. Did I actually think this was a hot item last spring?"

"If I remember correctly, you were working the punch and cookie table at the prom, studying for your SATs behind the bowl most of the evening. I don't think you were into chic last spring."

"*You* were. You looked great in that jacket at the prom. Still do. Boy, last spring I didn't even consider us as a possibility. Of course, you were otherwise *occupado*."

"Yeah, and I've got a real feeling Jordan's looking to recreate the past tonight. I've got to talk to her, Sue. I've got to tell her our situation. I think she thinks there's some chance of her and me getting back together."

"Not from anything you've said?"

"No. Of course not. You don't still worry about that, do you?"

"Oh, a little, once in a while. You know, I guess I worry that something will trigger the old magic and sweep you away."

"Well, get that out of your head. That only happens in those historical romances you read. Jordan and I just sort of happened. Like spontaneous combustion. She was there and I was there and everybody thought we were such a cute couple and we started believing it, too. We romanced each other six ways from Sunday, but I don't think either of us ever got as far as actually loving the other."

Jordan's sitting in the shadows, on the top row of bleachers, her back pressed against the cinder block wall. She's watching everybody dance. She's a self-created wallflower. If she wanted, she could be dancing with any of the guys who wanted to dance with her at the prom, when she was dancing every dance with Graham. Tonight, too, he's the only one she wants to dance with. Not every number. Just one slow dance. If her plan works, that ought to be enough.

He's dancing with Sue now. Reluctantly. Jordan can see that even from this distance. Graham hates to dance. Or at least pretends to hate it. When forced into it, he just makes fun of the whole idea by dancing really terribly, like someone who learned by mail, from lessons with footprint sheets. Clod-hop-hop-turn-dip. Shaking his hands like maracas all the while. Sue is just ignoring this and dancing like a regular human being.

There aren't many slow dances. This is a crowd heavily into rock. Jordan has to wait almost an hour for her chance, but it finally comes. The lights go from red and yellow to deep blue, and the crowd rearranges itself — fast dancers leaving, slow dancers edging onto the floor.

Jordan's a slow dancer. She just doesn't have her partner yet. She will. She's going to make this a personal Ladies' Choice.

Graham and Sue have stayed on the floor. When Jordan comes up, they're cheek-to-cheek, eyes closed dreamily. It's a scene few would have the nerve to break into. But Jordan knows she won't have many chances. She has to go for it.

She taps Sue lightly on the shoulder.

Sue turns and, seeing it's Jordan, smiles.

"Ladies' Choice," Jordan lies.

"Oh," Sue says, surprised. "Sure. You can

have him. He's more cooperative on slow numbers, but he's still more trouble than he's worth on the dance floor."

"Jordan," Graham says. "Just the girl I wanted to talk to. Come away with me — " he does a little Fred Astaire spin " — and we'll trip the light fantastic."

For a few moments, they just dance. Neither of them says anything. It's an old song with a heavy four-four beat. Jordan tightens her arms around Graham and moves into the music. She can feel the old chemistry working between them. They're dancing like one creature, not two separate beings. He must feel this, too. No matter what little college romance he's had going with Sue, he must feel the ultimate rightness of him and Jordan.

Completely caught up in her own mood, she puts her mouth against his ear and whispers, "I'm still in love with you."

"Oh Jordan," Graham moans, not knowing what he can say that won't hurt her, not even knowing how he can start to turn this conversation around.

She takes his "Oh Jordan" to be the lead-in to "Oh Jordan, I still love you, too." Thinking they're both on the same wavelength, she rushes on.

"I was a fool to leave. What happiness have I found in New York? I didn't know I had everything I wanted right here with you. But you will forgive me, won't you? You will give us another chance, won't you?"

Graham pulls back from her and looks at her eyes. They're brimming with tears. This isn't just a Jordan ploy. He can see she really means it. He doesn't know what to do, where to begin.

"Let's go outside," he says. "It looks like the rain's stopped. We can walk around the cinder track for old time's sake. We can't really talk in here, and it looks like we need to talk."

I've got him! Jordan thinks. *Once we're out there in the moonlight, alone, one kiss and everything will be back where it left off.*

He guides her through the crowd by her arm. She's in front of him and so doesn't see him signaling Sue with a nod as they leave the gym. They get outside. The rain has stopped, leaving the night wrapped in a moon-lit mist.

They walk behind the school, around to where the football field and running track are. The lights are on, throwing the night into white relief.

Walking around the track side-by-side, Graham kicks cinders with the toe of his shoe, trying to find a way into this hard conversation.

"Jordan. You said a lot back there. Now it's my turn."

"Okay, darling."

He winces. This is going worse than he imagined. He puts his arm around her shoulder to soften his words.

"You went to New York and lived there

nearly a year. A lot happened to you there. You're a different person now than you were when you left. It's the same with me. I wasn't just sitting in place all that time. I went away to school. I studied and played golf and nursed my broken heart over you."

"Oh Graham," Jordan says, starting to cry, "I'm so sorry. I'll make it up to you. I promise."

"Please," he says. "Just let me finish."

"Okay," she sniffles.

"One of the things that happened to me up there was that I fell in love. With Sue."

"On the rebound," Jordan inserts.

"Maybe. It doesn't matter. It's real love. And part of our love is that we became lovers."

"Oh Graham. I don't care about that. Do you think I've been in a convent in New York?"

"Jordan. Please."

"Okay, okay. Sorry."

"Well, the thing is, that now there's another person in the scenario."

"I know," Jordan says, smiling.

"No. Not you. Someone smaller."

Jordan looks at him, confused.

"Sue's pregnant. We're going to have a baby. If she'll have me — and I'm hoping she will — we're going to get married. I'm going to be a house-husband/day care center/diaper changer/part-time golfer while Sue becomes one of America's great architects. I know you had something else in mind, but maybe you can see it from a slightly different angle. Maybe as one of our best friends, you can be happy for us. Maybe . . ." he goes on, but Jordan isn't listening. She isn't even there. She's running off the track, around the school.

First he lets her go. He can't really think of anything to say to make her come back. Nothing he wants to say anyway. And so he just stands there for a little while. And then he starts wondering where she's gone to, and what she's going to do. He knows she's really upset. And not just about him. He can tell she's not in a good place right now, that she's depressed about too many things. She probably shouldn't be left alone right now. She might do something. No, she wouldn't, he decides. Then as rapidly he changes his mind, and starts to run after her, shouting into the night beyond the track lights, "Jordan!"

Chapter 14

Graham turns and rushes back into the school, running down the hall toward the gym. He takes the darkened stairs two at a time up into the balcony and leans over the railing looking down at the couples below, dancing to an old Blondie number that Eddie and the Losers are murdering.

He scans back and forth across the floor, knowing all the while that he won't find Jordan here. She was way too upset to just come back in and slide out onto the dance floor.

He does see Sue, though. She's off in a corner talking with the Malone sisters. Although at first it seems impossible, Graham keeps staring until he's sure his eyes aren't deceiving him. One of the Malone sisters — in a ruffled prom dress — is holding a basketball. Worse, she's dribbling a basketball. It looks like she's demonstrating some refinement of technique to Sue.

Graham rushes downstairs and comes into

the gym through the entrance closest to where Sue is.

". . . We call it digital dribbling," the Malone sister — Graham can't tell which one it is — is telling Sue when he gets there.

"Sorry," he says, breathless, "got to steal my girl for a minute." He takes Sue by the hand and then, from the look he's getting from the Malone, realizes it's the second time this weekend he's done this.

When he and Sue get out into the hall, he gives her a fast outline of what happened out on the cinder track. Sue listens and nods.

"We'll find her," Sue says with assurance, putting a hand on Graham's shoulder to calm him down. "You did the right thing. It would have been worse to let her go on thinking there was a possibility of you two getting back together. She had to find out sooner or later what's really going on. And the later you let it get, the larger she probably would've built her fantasy."

"But you didn't see the pain on her face just before she ran off. It was awful," Graham says, edginess in his voice.

"We'll find her. My guess is she's where girls who are upset usually hide out — the ladies' room. I'll check all of them. Meanwhile, why don't you go back outside and look in all the nooks and crannies where she might be hiding out."

"What *are* crannies anyway?" Graham stops in his tracks. He does this a lot — gets momentarily diverted by something completely irrelevant. "Do they always go with nooks, or do you ever find a cranny just out on its own?"

Sue gives him a friendly shove. She knows it's pretty easy to get him back in gear.

"Deep philosophical questions will have to wait. We've got a missing Jordan to find."

"I'm on my way," he says, and is.

He goes down the long hall of school, to get to the other side, where the pool is. Jordan always used to sneak in there for midnight swims. Maybe she's cooling out in the deep end tonight.

The hall is so dark that Graham almost misses Scooter and Leigh. The other reason he almost misses them is because they are making out with each other. Something he has never seen them do before.

Doing a double take, Graham stops so fast the rubber soles of his running shoes squeak loud enough to startle Leigh and Scooter. They both look up.

"Uh, hi, old buddy," Scooter says.

"Hi Graham," Leigh says shyly.

"Remind me later to ask you two what's happening here. I don't seem to be quite up to the minute. Right now, though, can you help me look for Jordan? I told her about me and Sue and the baby and she did not take the news terrifically well."

"Where did you leave her?" Leigh asks.

"Out on the running track. But she could be anywhere by now. Sue's looking in the girls' johns. I was heading for the pool. Maybe you two could look around outside. Why don't we meet back here in, say, fifteen minutes? If we don't find her by then, we can get the cars and look further. She might've just gone home, but I doubt it. You know how Jordan feels about her parents. I don't think she'd want them to see her really upset. She'd have to do a whole lot of explaining, and I'm sure she'd hate that."

When Scooter and Leigh get outside, he turns to her and says, "Don't let me forget where we left off back there."

"Are you kidding? It only took me years to get you there. There's no way I'm going to let you go now that I've got you where I want you."

"In the vampire's clutches," he says, backing off, flipping his collar up. "Oh well, I'll die bloodless, but with a smile on my face." He gets suddenly serious. "Leigh. You don't think Jordan would do anything dumb, do you?"

"Like? Give me category. You're thinking of something specific, aren't you?"

"I'm probably being an alarmist."

"Scott. You're never an alarmist. If you think she might be doing something crazy, she probably is. Now tell me."

"Well, she's got a lot of speed. Some quack in New York has her and her friends loaded up with diet pills. She's pretty strung out. If she gulped a whole bottle — to try to off herself, or just to get Graham's attention — she could do some damage."

"Let's get going. You go up to the second floor. I'll check out the parking lot. If she's looking to do herself in, she'll have to be someplace where she's got a little privacy."

They split up and take off. Scooter goes through every classroom on the second floor. Sue checks every girls' john. Graham gets down to the pool and throws the lights on. The surface of the water is like glass. No one's been in there for some time.

Leigh is out in the parking lot, which is full of cars because of the dance. And since Scooter chivalrously dropped her and Jordan at the door when they arrived in the storm, she doesn't know where he parked his car.

At first she wanders frantically in one direction, then another, calling out Jordan's name as she goes. After a while, she realizes she's retracing her steps. She has, in fact, passed the same red Corvette three times.

She stops herself and tries to think this through.

I should start at one end, go through each row, look at every car.

It's starting to rain again, which makes the job harder. Leigh's in high heels — an unusual state of being for her feet — and loses footing a couple of times on the slick asphalt. And so she has to go slower. Which means getting wetter.

Finally, after what seems like two days, but is probably more like fifteen minutes, she spots Scooter's car wedged between two vans. The rain is starting to really come down now. The car windows are all closed and blurred over. She can't see at first if anyone's inside. She wipes away the rain with the palms of her hands.

"Jordan! Jordan, are you in there?"

She stops. She thinks she hears something. Something very faint. Singing.

"We all live in a yellow submarine. A yellow submarine. A yellow submarine."

"Jordan! Open up!"

Leigh peers in and sees Jordan laughing back at her flamboyantly, as if she's just told the best joke.

"That's right," Leigh says. "Hahaha. A great joke. Now let old Leigh in so we can laugh at it together."

Jordan grows suddenly difficult.

"No," she says, like a nine-year-old brat.

"Jordan," Leigh says, straining every bit of fury out of her voice so that it comes out almost kindly, "let me in there, or I'll have to pull every single one of those blond hairs out of your head."

Click.

Jordan has pulled up the door lock pin.

Leigh opens it and jumps inside, into the backseat where Jordan is sprawled and now crying.

"He's going to have her baby!"

Leigh lets this lapse in basic biology slide by. She knows what Jordan means.

"Ruined everything. Whole life down the tubes. Only guy I'll ever love. Gonna drive away in yellow submarine." She's half talking, half singing. She's extremely agitated, her hands flying in every direction as she talks. She's fidgeting restlessly in the seat, runs her hands wildly through her hair.

"Jordan, listen to me," Leigh says, taking her friend's face between her hands, trying to hold her attention long enough to get an answer to what she figures is the most important question of the moment.

"Have you taken any pills?"

"Pills," Jordan says.

"Yes. Diet pills."

"Dr. Don's pills?" Jordan says and begins giggling, and pulls an amber plastic prescription bottle out of her purse. She turns it upside down to show it's empty. *"All gone,"* she says redundantly, and then lapses back into the theme song of the evening.

"We all live in a — "

"Yellow submarine, yes," Leigh fills in for her. "Look, Jor, just stay here in the sub for a minute. I'm going to go get Captain Scooter. He can take us for a ride."

She gets out of the car, wondering how she's ever going to find him. Then she remembers he's covering the second floor. She rushes back into the school and up the stairs and finds him in the third room she tries.

She's so out of breath she can't get any words out. But he figures out what she's trying to say anyway.

"You've found her?"

Leigh nods.

"Show me."

By the time they get back to the car, Jordan is on to singing "I Am the Walrus." She seems more disoriented, more disconnected. She doesn't really seem to know who Scooter and Leigh are, or that they're even there.

Scooter leans into the backseat and looks into Jordan's eye, holding the lids apart. Then he puts his fingers on her wrist and takes her pulse.

"Let's go," he says quickly, getting his car key out and sliding into the driver's seat. Leigh gets in the other side.

"Where?" she asks.

"She needs an emergency room. I just hope she doesn't need it faster than we can get her there."

Chapter 15

Scooter smashes the gearshift into first and floors the old Ford out of the parking lot. Leigh climbs over into the backseat and wedges in next to Jordan to prop her up. She's now babbling incoherently and flopping around like a marionette on loose strings.

When they come around the front of the school, Leigh spots Graham and Sue coming out the front doors.

"Hospital!" Leigh shouts out the open back window. At the speed Scooter's going, there really isn't time for much more of an explanation. She tacks on a fast impersonation of an ambulance siren for emphasis, then feels foolish. This still happens once in a while. She'll go on too long with a joke or a set of directions, or wind up covering the same ground in a story twice. This stuff doesn't happen as often as it used to, though, and Leigh thinks a lot of it wasn't her slowness or dumbness as much as her lack of sureness that anyone was really listening to her.

Graham waves and nods to show he understands what's going on. He and Sue head for the parking lot, probably to get the Fiat and follow, Leigh figures.

"*Do you know the muffin man, the muffin man, the muffin man,*" Jordan is singing now, a song she probably hasn't sung since she was five. She looks over at Leigh and focuses in. Sort of.

"I know you," she says.

"Right, I'm Leigh."

Jordan nods. "Leigh," she says, as if committing it to memory. "We're going for a ride on the roller coaster?" she says with a child-like note of hope in her voice.

"No," Leigh says, putting her arm around Jordan's shoulders, which are both sweaty and cold, "you've already been on the roller coaster. Now we're going to try to get you off." She pulls an old cotton sweater of Scooter's off the floor and wraps Jordan up in it.

"She getting weird?" Scooter says over his shoulder.

"Megaweird," Leigh says.

"Well, we're almost there," Scooter says, tearing down Pine Street toward Jamesburg General Hospital. He overshoots the emergency entrance, and so screeches to a stop, throws the car into reverse, backs up the fifty feet or so to the drive, then whips the car around and peels up it.

"Wheee!" Jordan shouts with delight. "We *are* on the roller coaster!"

"That's right, Jor," Scooter says. "It's Six Flags Over Jamesburg. And here comes the next ride — the Wild Wheelchair!"

An orderly is heading out toward them with one.

"Graham and Sue must've called ahead," Leigh says.

The orderly pulls Jordan out of the backseat — very gently — and sits her down in the wheelchair.

"What've we got here?" The orderly, who is around twenty-five and blond, looks like a minor character in an afternoon soap.

"Dexedrine," Scooter says, handing him the empty bottle.

"You know how many were in here when she started?"

Scooter shakes his head.

"Ooooh, you're cute!" Jordan says, reaching out and running her hand in a quick, flippy way through the orderly's hair. Then, just as quickly as she focused in on him, she tunes to another station and says, "I think I'm going to be sick."

"Best think that could happen to you," the orderly says, stepping up his pace to get her inside. And then he and Jordan are gone in a flash, beyond the double swinging doors.

Leigh and Scooter turn at the same moment to the sound of tires wooshing on the wet pavement of the hospital parking lot. It's Graham and Sue.

They've figured out the basics of what happened, but want the details. Scooter and Leigh fill them in.

"I feel rotten," Graham says. "Why couldn't I have found some way of telling her that would've given her a way out. No, Clodface here has to kick her in the teeth with the news."

"Stop," Scooter says. "We all tried to clue her in gently, but it didn't work. She wouldn't listen. She didn't want to. Somebody had to tell her the truth sooner or later. I guess it just finally fell to you. She'll get over her heartbreak — I mean, Graham, it's only you we're talking about here, not Mel Gibson."

In response to this, Graham punches Scooter in the arm. Some of the old Stamper ways of talking and dealing with each other haven't changed in all their years together. This one dates back to about third grade. "All I'm hoping is that she'll live to *have* a broken heart."

Chapter 16

There isn't a real waiting room in the emergency station of Jamesburg General — just an old coffee machine and a row of hinged-together green plastic chairs.

One of these chairs is empty. One is occupied by a guy in a Maytag repair jumpsuit waiting for his wife. She slipped coming up the slick front steps of their house and put her hand through the storm door. He brought her in — her hand wrapped in a towel gone red with blood — and has been waiting here for the half hour since they took her in.

The other four chairs are taken up by four-fifths of the Stamp Club, who've been waiting close to an hour now for word on Jordan.

"I'll ask again at the reception desk," Sue says.

"I wouldn't if I were you," Scooter says. "That nurse is a direct descendant of Attila the Hun. *Mean.* When I went up last time, she told me if we bothered her again, she'd bite our ankles."

"Now why do I have the feeling that is a complete fabrication?" Graham says.

"Well, she *did* give me a pretty heavy glare. She said they'll tell us when they know anything."

"Is there really a chance Jordan won't make it?" Leigh says in a low voice. Scooter takes her hand and says, "Depends how many pills she took. No one knows how many were left in the bottle when she decided to make a late-night snack out of them."

"What do you think they're doing to her in there?" Sue asks.

"Nothing fun probably," Graham says. He stands up and goes over to the coffee machine, puts in two quarters, and pushes buttons for coffee, cream, and sugar. Nothing happens. He waits. More nothing happens. Ordinarily, Graham is the mildest mannered person on earth. Now, though, he takes his size thirteen foot and kicks the machine so hard its lights go out and its wheeze-hum sound abruptly dies.

"You killed it," Scooter says, coming over and pressing his ear to the silent metal hulk.

"You okay?" Sue asks Graham.

He shakes his head.

"I just feel so responsible." He begins to cry.

It's Leigh who stops him.

"Look," she says, getting up and going over and bringing him back, by the hand, to the chairs, "if Jordan comes out of this and still wants you back, would you go?"

Graham looks up, shocked.

"No. I love Sue."

"So. You can't give Jordan what she wants. The thing is, I'm not sure she really wants it."

"No?" Graham says.

"Oh, I think she cared about you more than she let on. All along. But she couldn't let you see that, and so it never really happened between you two. But now, I think she's just drowning in a million regrets. You're just the one regret she's focused on."

"Yeah," Scooter says, taking off his tux jacket and shirt, peeling down to the sleeveless black T-shirt underneath. It's stifling in the airless hallway. "She's depressed about New York, too. It just didn't pan out like she hoped. I know what that's like from California. You pin your dreams on a place. But places don't save you."

"What does then?" Sue wonders.

"Well, friends maybe," Leigh says. "I've talked to Jordan about coming up to Maine with me this summer. I think a lot of what's wrong is she thinks she's missed all her chances, and bungled everything, and has nowhere to go. I think if someone can toss her a lifesaver, she'll grab on."

"Leigh," Sue says, putting an arm around her shoulders, "you're really something."

Scooter stands up and fishes through his pockets, coming up with a few bills and a little change.

"Since this coffee machine seems to be a

dead issue, why don't I run over to the Lunchbox and get us all some? I feel so powerless just sitting here."

"I'll go along," Leigh offers.

Right after Leigh and Scooter have gone, the wife of the Maytag guy comes out properly bandaged, but looking very pale. He takes her by her good arm and leads her out, turning just before he goes to tell Graham and Sue, "Hope it goes okay for your friend."

"Thanks," they say. Then when he's out the door they simultaneously grin sheepishly.

"I completely forgot he was there," Sue says.

"I guess he heard everything. We probably ought to make him an honorary Stamper."

Sue takes Graham's hands, one in each of her own, and looks down at them.

"This whole night has really opened my eyes in so many ways. Jordan in there." She nods toward the closed doors to the emergency room. "I think, what if she doesn't pull through? I've been thinking everything's going to go on the same, but maybe it won't. Things can change drastically in a moment. And then I've been thinking about Scooter and Leigh, who nearly missed each other. They probably wouldn't have happened if one or the other of them hadn't come back to the reunion. The fates are just so unpredictable."

"Why do I get this feeling you're trying to tell me something?" Graham teases.

"I am doing a pretty pitiful job of coming to the point, aren't I? Well, it's just that all of a sudden I see that whatever surprises come along in *my* life, I want to have you there to share them with. And I don't want to pass you up this time, because who knows — there might not be a next. So," she says, spinning out of the chair, down onto one knee, "will you plight me thy troth? Will you marry me?"

Graham grabs her up into his arms, pulls her to him, and says softly into her ear, "Well, when our grandkids ask how I proposed, we'll have an interesting story to tell them."

Suddenly there's a metallic bang as the emergency room doors swing open and the tall doctor who took Jordan in, emerges.

Graham and Sue break out of their clinch and look at him expectantly.

"She'll be okay," he says. "I want her here tonight, but just so we can keep an eye on her. We pumped her stomach, so she should be coming down pretty soon. She's going to have a hell of a headache for a few hours, but otherwise she shouldn't be too much the worse for wear. I want to talk with her and her parents, though. About the Dexedrine, and about what's wrong with her life that makes her need to take it every day, and occasionally by the bottleful. Did you call them like I asked you?"

"We thought we'd wait until we found out how she was," Graham says.

"Yeah," Sue says, "we didn't want to alarm them if we didn't have to."

The doctor fixes them with a stern glare. "When there's trouble, you have to notify the next of kin."

"Well," Graham shrugs. "That's us. That's the Stampers."

Chapter 17

"Is she awake?" Sue asks the doctor.

"Mmmhmm," he says, "but she's pretty weak."

"Can we see her for a minute?"

"One of you can go in," he says. "The other can call her parents."

"I'd like to go," Sue says to Graham. He nods and gives her hand a squeeze as she pushes through the double doors.

The emergency room is one large space filled with all sorts of medical machinery and equipment, and a desk with two nurses sitting at it and an orderly sitting *on* it, eating a sandwich. Lining the walls are half a dozen beds, each with curtains that can be pulled around them. All the beds are empty, the curtains open, except one. Sue walks across the room toward it.

She pulls the curtain aside a little and goes in. Jordan's eyes are closed, but she opens them at the sound of Sue coming in.

"Hi," she says in a much smaller than usual Jordan voice.

"Hi," Sue says and pulls the visitor's chair around so she can sit close. "How awful do you feel?"

"Well, I would *not* put getting my stomach pumped in the highlight reel of my life. Boy, I really made a mess of the night, didn't I?"

"At least you didn't die. That would've been a drag on the whole weekend." Stamper talk.

"Don't you dare make me laugh. It hurts when I even smile," Jordan says, then gets serious again. "I heard about the baby. I was thinking he'll be the first second-generation Stamper."

"*She*," Sue says, which makes both of them smile.

"You and Graham," Jordan says. "It's a good thing, eh?"

Sue nods.

"I'm sorry about last night," Jordan says. "About the whole weekend really."

"It's okay," Sue says, reaching out and smoothing Jordan's hair off her tired face. "We don't have to talk about it. I know you're not exactly in top form at the moment."

"Okay," Jordan says with a weak smile of gratitude. "But I needed to apologize, to let you know I was just acting out of a crazy moment. And to thank you— all the Stampers really — for rescuing me. Boy, if I'd actually managed to kill myself, I would've been really upset."

Both of them realize at the same moment what an absurd statement this is, and break into grins.

"Oh no," Jordan says, "I can't laugh." She holds still for a moment until she can get serious, then says to Sue, "Listen. The other thing is that I won't be hanging around to bother you and Graham this summer. Leigh's convinced me that the great outdoors of Maine are just what I need to put the color back in my cheeks. You know — fresh air and sunshine and an early bedtime. I guess it's pretty obvious I could use a little of that."

"Sounds like a good plan," Sue says.

Yeah, Jordan thinks, when Sue has gone. *A good plan. But Sue doesn't know the half of it. Not the tenth of it. Going to Maine is just Step One. I can get my act together up there. Then in the fall I'll head back to New York. With all my experience now, I can make a heavy duty assault on Broadway. I'll get a new prescription from Dr. Don. I can handle the pills this time. I'll just take them every other day. The rest of the time I'll just starve myself on sheer willpower. I'll make it to every casting call, even if it means going on no sleep at all. I can do it. I can do what it takes to make it. And then, when my name's up there in lights, then Graham will want me back.*

Chapter 18

Wednesday morning Scooter — always the hungriest Stamper — is the first to show up at the Lunchbox Café, where the five of them have planned to meet before heading off in various directions.

As he comes through the door, Marion, who has run the Lunchbox for as long as Scooter can remember, calls out from behind the counter, "Hey! Scooter!"

"Scott," he corrects her wearily. He's about ready to give up on his name change, just from the effort of constantly setting everybody straight. Leigh's after him, though, to keep on with the plan.

"Okay. Scott," Marion says. "Me, I don't care what you call me, just so you don't call me late for dinner."

Scooter thinks of Marion as the ultimate waitress. It's hard to imagine her as anything else, hard to envision her in a regular dress, as opposed to her white polyester waitress dress with the starched purple handkerchief pinned in a fan shape under her MARION name tag.

Marion has been dishing up eggs at breakfast and meat loaf at lunch, and coffee all day long since Scooter was a little boy. Everything stays the same in the Lunchbox Café — the worn old linoleum floor, the checked curtains at the windows, the chrome and glass case filled with slices of Marion's homemade pies. He likes this, finds it reassuring. Too much else has changed for him.

During the year he was on his own, living up in the Stamp Pad, Scooter came over to the Lunchbox almost every day. Marion always says she's going to put a little commemorative plaque on his stool at the counter, that he now has Lifetime Member status at the Lunchbox.

"I wish you'd move the Lunchbox out to California," he tells her now, as she slides a heavy mug of coffee with cream across the counter at him.

"You just got here and now you're going back already?" she says, handing him an old typed menu in a yellowed plastic folder.

"Maybe not forever, but yeah, I've got some loose ends I want to tie up there."

The old screen door slams behind him. Scooter turns to see Sue, who looks like an extra from *Night of the Zombies*. She is the slowest waker-upper in America. She sleepwalks over to the counter, gropes her way onto a stool, peers at Marion through half-closed eyes and says, in a raspy voice, "Coff . . ."

"One cuppa java coming up!" Marion booms, and Sue's eyes pop open as if someone just crashed together a couple of cymbals. Then, as soon as Marion has turned around to get the coffee pot, Sue leans against Scooter, her head on his shoulder, and begins snoring.

"Maybe we ought to give this to her intravenously," Marion says, pouring the cup full of coffee. She picks up the cup and moves it back and forth under Sue's nose. The eyes open again, and Sue takes the cup and begins drinking. When she's drained half the cup, she looks around, like Dorothy just noticing she's arrived in Oz.

"Where is everybody?"

"You and I are the first arrivals at this little farewell. I hope they show up pretty soon. I want to make tracks today. I've got a lot of miles to cover."

"Why are you going back to California?" Sue says, holding out the empty coffee cup toward Marion like Oliver Twist in the orphanage. "I thought you weren't that crazy about it out there. And what about you and Leigh? Why don't you go up to Maine with her?"

"Sue. You know me and the great out-of-doors and wildlife and all that. To me, nature is what you drive through on your way to the Holiday Inn. Besides, Leigh can't rescue everyone at once. She's going to have plenty on her hands this summer with Jordan. And double besides, I need to go back to California to try to do it right this time. I'm going to stop just hacking around and really get down to business on my music."

"But I thought you and Leigh. . . ."

"We figure if what we've got is as good as we think it is, it'll keep for a few months. She's going to come out and see me for a couple of weeks in August. Maybe she'll like California. Maybe she'll persuade me to come back and be the biggest rock star in Dunbar, Maine. Anything's possible. Maybe we'll just be one of those trendy bicoastal couples. Jetting across the country to see each other."

Leigh has come in unnoticed while Scooter's talking, in time to hear the tail end of what he's saying.

"Yeah," she says, coming up behind Scooter, putting her hands on his shoulders, "everything else about this romance has been weird and unexpected and impossible. Why should we suddenly get normal about anything?" She looks around. "Hey Marion. Can we take the big table in the back? There's going to be five of us eventually."

"Six," Sue says, patting her stomach. She picks up her coffee mug and follows Leigh and Scooter toward the table Marion has indicated with a wave of her dishcloth.

It's a truly glorious New England summer morning and all the windows in the Lunchbox are wide open, which lets in all the bird chirps and shouts of kids on their way to school, and the hiss of tiny metal wheels running over sidewalk. Skateboard wheels.

Scooter notices them first, turns and looks out the window to see Graham's head glide by. Half a minute later it glides by again in the opposite direction, grinning in at them.

"Looks like juvenile delinquency is back on the streets of Jamesburg," Leigh says.

"The responsible, mature, adult father of my child," Sue says, just as the screen door springs open and Graham comes crashing through, doing a wheelie the length of the restaurant, stopping on a dime about six inches short of the table.

"And to think," Scooter says, "Marion doesn't even have a cover charge for all this entertainment."

"So," Graham says, "the gang's all here."

"Except Jordan," Leigh says. "I hope she's finished packing. It's a long day's drive up to Maine and I want to get started pretty soon."

"Wait a minute," Graham says, seeing her coming down the sidewalk. "Here she is!" He stands and pantomimes a Johnny Carson golf swing. "Here's Jordan!"

Jordan, who has spent the past few days in her backyard, lying low, tanning her way back to her old self, pulls up a chair and passes a wide grin around the table. Then she just sits there in silence for a long moment.

"Boy, do I love you guys," she says, her

eyes filling with tears. She looks around the table at all of them, careful not to let her loving gaze linger on Graham longer than on any of the others. "Would somebody help me out and change the subject?" she says. "If I start in telling you all how much you mean to me, I'll just get all soppy and embarrass myself and all of you."

She pulls a paper napkin out of the table dispenser and wipes her eyes, then looks around for Marion. When she spots her, Jordan shouts, "Hey! Can you whip up a plate of scrambled eggs and sausage and home fries and an English muffin and a big glass of o.j. for a starving Stamper?"

"What's this?" Sue says. "Jordan eating? Real food?"

"Oh, why not?" Jordan says, laughing. "If I'm going to be leading this hearty outdoor life, lumberjacking, or whatever it is Leigh's got me signed up for, I guess I can afford a few extra calories." But behind the laugh, she's thinking, *Sure I can. I'll just have to get back on Dr. Don's program when I get to New York. Maybe I'll even have to take the pills every day. But just for a while. Just to get started.*

"I don't know about you," Graham says to Sue, "but I'm getting depressed. Leigh and Jordan off to the wilds of Maine. Scooter — Scott — off to the wilds of southern California while we look forward to a summer at the exciting Jamesburg Garden Center."

"Building the nest egg," Sue says. "Working for Graham's dad. But I don't really mind sticking around here. This may be my last summer in Jamesburg and I find myself sort of missing all the old places already. The summer'll give me a chance to hold on to my adolescence for a couple more months. Before I parachute into adulthood."

"When's the baby due?" Scooter asks.

"Looks like January," Sue says. "We'll have to initiate her into the Stamp Club as soon as she's born."

"Boy," Graham says, shaking his head, "the Stamp Club has been through its own initiation, hasn't it? But we've survived. With all that's happened, we're still together."

"Oh no," Scooter says. "We're getting sentimental. I never thought I'd live to see it happen. But clearly it has. And it probably means we're edging toward the next step, the one we've held back from for all these years."

"What?" Leigh says.

"Getting T-shirts printed."

The five of them laugh so hard and all at once that Marion comes out of the kitchen to see what's going on.

"Now why can't you behave yourselves? Like that nice bunch from the Spanish Club?"

Summer Blockbusters!

Books chosen with you in mind from

point™
—Pass the word.

Living...loving...growing.
That's what **POINT** books are all about!
They're books you'll love reading and
will want to tell your friends about.

Don't miss these other exciting **Point** titles!

NEW POINT TITLES! $2.25 each

☐ QI 33306-2 **The Karate Kid** B.B. Hiller
☐ QI 31987-6 **When We First Met** Norma Fox Mazer
☐ QI 32512-4 **Just the Two of Us** Hila Colman
☐ QI 32338-5 **If This Is Love, I'll Take Spaghetti** Ellen Conford
☐ QI 32728-3 **Hello...Wrong Number** Marilyn Sachs
☐ QI 33216-3 **Love Always, Blue** Mary Pope Osborne
☐ QI 33116-7 **The Ghosts of Departure Point** Eve Bunting
☐ QI 33195-7 **How Do You Lose Those Ninth Grade Blues?** Barthe DeClements
☐ QI 33550-2 **Charles in Charge** Elizabeth Faucher
☐ QI 32306-7 **Take It Easy** Steven Kroll
☐ QI 33409-3 **Slumber Party** Christopher Pike